# *Midley*

# Five Gold Coins

## Emma Batten

To Jane!
Happy reading!
Emma

First published in the UK by Emma Batten

Printed by PWP, Hastings

ISBN 978-1-7399854-5-5

Edited by Debbie Rigden

Further editing and proofreading by Liz Hopkin & Maud Matley

Cover painting by Kean Farrelly

www.emmabattenauthor.com

For Debbie,

I dedicate this Midley series to you, with thanks for all the inconsistencies you spot, your amazing ability to recall what I have, or have not, written in earlier chapters, and for sharing your local knowledge with me.

You have supported me and my writing from the very beginning, first as a reader and then editor, and I love working with you as each new story comes to life.

# Introduction

Welcome to the second in my series inspired by a lost settlement named Midley on Romney Marsh. The stories are stand-alone, so no need to read them in order.

Come with me all the way back to 14th century Canterbury and Romney Marsh. My historical characters are all fictional. Only the incident involving the Archbishop of Canterbury is true, but the response from my characters and the aftermath are all imaginary. As always, I am trying to make the area recognisable and to be historically accurate, while bringing the tale to life.

Towards the end we move on to the 21st century. The characters and scenes are real. Thank you to Phil and Joan Castle for sharing their story with me and allowing me to add to it with my own story.

But first, let's go to Canterbury in the year 1381...

# *Diggory*

## Canterbury
## 15th June 1381

The city of Canterbury is my place. My home. When I dust myself down at the end of the day, I feel proud to be part of its story.

As a stonemason, I have spent these past six years working on West Gate, so it now stands stronger than ever before. Working with stone runs in my blood and, whichever way I turn, I will see a brother... a cousin... an uncle labouring nearby. We have been so absorbed with the city gateway that people now refer to us by the name Western. Diggory Western I have become, and it suits me well.

At the top of West Gate, I have carved my mark and hope it remains there for centuries to come. From here, gazing outwards across the Stour, a straight road leads into the countryside and the city's farmland that provides us with food. It is a busy thoroughfare with a flow of country people leading horses with wagons, pushing handcarts or carrying baskets across the drawbridge. I hear their chatter, the squawk of their birds, the grunt of their pigs, the maa of their goats and I know that a life working on the city boundaries will never be peaceful.

Those countryfolk pour through the gateway not long after daybreak, hopeful of selling their produce at the market. Later, strangers come, wide-eyed with wonder. Although two centuries have passed since Archbishop Thomas Beckett was murdered in the crypt of our glorious cathedral, pilgrims are still called to visit his shrine. As I work on West Gate, I too am drawn to the cathedral. Amongst the city's ragstone and flint, thatch and tiles, its towers glow a glorious pale gold.

The stone comes from Caen in Normandy – a fine-grained, creamy-yellow limestone. Its texture allows the cathedral masons to carve intricate tracery, chevron mouldings and lifelike corbels with precision. On a quiet summer's evening, I wander around the southern side of the nave and marvel at the restoration carried out by those master masons. What a fine thing it would have been to serve an apprenticeship working with Caen stone, but that is not for the Westerns. We know our place and to work on the city gates and walls in local ragstone is worthy employment.

Sometimes I imagine that within the sacred walls of that holy place, the steward spends his days counting the money that pours into his coffers. I wonder if, every now and then, the copper and the silver are exchanged for gold. And perhaps the steward counts the gold, or perhaps he keeps his accounts so well that he knows exactly how much flows into the cathedral dedicated to Jesus Christ our Saviour.

Looking inwards from my gate, I can see crowds of people and a maze of shops, homes and church towers. From one place – the spot where I carved my mason's mark – I can see the thatched roof of the cottage I share with my two brothers, Mark and Paul, Mark's wife and three young children. Across the street, the patch of fresh straw on my parents' cottage roof is easily visible. Our homes nestle behind the newly built Holy Cross church, a mere stone's throw from my West Gate and laboured upon by the many branches of my mother's family.

Towards the north, the city walls are being repaired. By the time the leaves are changing colour, I will be working on those walls and, stone by stone, flint by flint, my work will take me further from West Gate and towards North Gate.

This afternoon, our work has been interrupted by the tolling of the death knell from the cathedral. It distracted us from our work as we wondered what it heralded. News flows quickly from the cathedral to the rest of the city, and we knew it would not be long before we learnt the reason for the repetitive ring of one bell. But when that news came, it shocked every one of us.

"It's Archbishop Sudbury!" my brother Mark told me as we passed on the stone stairs of West Gate. "Murdered in London!"

"Murdered?" I repeated, my tone hushed. "It can't be true."

Yet it was. As the afternoon progressed, more details came. "It was because of the tax," my uncle said as we walked to the alehouse to quench our thirst on the warm summer's evening. "There's some fellow who rebelled against it and they sought out the person who thought of it – thought of the tax."

"But he's our archbishop," I countered. "It can't be true."

It was. The death knell from the cathedral confirmed it.

"Not anymore," my uncle retorted. "And he was Lord Chancellor too. That was his downfall."

"I wonder what will happen here." I waved my arm towards the Holy Cross Church and the city walls. "Archbishop Sudbury started all this... all these repairs, and they're not finished yet."

"It will be done," Mark said as he joined us, "and the cathedral too."

"There's no shortage of money in Canterbury," my uncle agreed. "Not while the pilgrims come."

"Will there be more miracles?" I wondered as we ducked our heads and entered the alehouse. "Will he become a martyr too?" But the long, low room was crowded, and it was near impossible to be heard clearly or to hear any response. "There will be changes, that is for certain," I murmured, mostly to myself.

# Brother Fabian

From the novices to the prior, we are all uneasy here in Christ Church Priory. We whisper when there should be silence. We pray when we should be working. Despite living under the Rule of St Benedict, each day following his set pattern, there is a feeling of not knowing what will happen next.

Archbishop Sudbury's body has been placed in a tomb in the northern side of the monks' quire of our cathedral. I say his body because his head is elsewhere – gone to his hometown in Suffolk. In its place there is a cannonball. We had to put something there.

A week has passed since the interment. For the meantime, we have ensured someone is praying for his soul day and night. The air in our lofty quire is thick with smoke from the flickering candles and filled with the fragrance of incense. As I move from quire to priory, the scents waft with me and settle in my treasury room which nestles on an upper floor between the cathedral and priory lodging rooms.

Earlier today, sitting at my oak desk, I heard the familiar heavy footsteps of Prior John on the stairway to my room. He rapped on the door and proceeded to press on the latch. At the open doorway he placed his hands together as if in prayer, bowing so his forehead touched upon his fingertips. "Let us bless the Lord."

I copied his gesture. "Thanks be to God."

"It has been a week," Prior John began. "Tomorrow I will ask that work on the rebuilding of the southern wall of the nave resumes. Archbishop Sudbury, God rest his soul, would want his good works completed."

"It would be his greatest wish," I agreed, lowering my gaze. "He gave much of his personal fortune to this project."

The late Archbishop Sudbury had taken Canterbury by storm. He kept an eye on every weakness in the city wall, every crumbling gateway or church, and was determined to restore and improve the city. To rebuild the cathedral nave was both ambitious and vital. Known as Lanfranc's Nave, built not long after the Normans came to Canterbury, it had been unsafe for decades. Now new walls were rising in the same Caen stone, and soaring window openings taking shape.

"It does no good for these masons to be idle," Prior John remarked.

I waited. He would be wanting money, I assumed. My coffers were full, despite the monumental work being undertaken in the nave.

"We will need money for the window lead and glass..." Prior John began. "But..." He eyed the locked chests. "There is plenty for other projects?"

"There is plenty."

"I am thinking of a place on Romney Marsh..."

Romney Marsh! All around us is God's land and not one place should be considered better or more worthy than the next, but I must confess to being surprised that the prior should be thinking of the outer reaches of the diocese at this time.

"It has been three years since the archbishop's last visitation of the area. Plans were drawn up to replace a wooden church at a place called Midley, not far from Romney and Lydd."

"A wooden church?" Now he had my full attention. "How can it be that Canterbury has a wooden church, however far away it is and however humble the settlement? We must serve our Lord the best we can, and Canterbury's glory should echo throughout the diocese." I stopped abruptly and muttered, "God forgive me for my pride."

Prior John, a gentle soul, responded with, "It is not pride, Brother Fabian. It is not Canterbury's glory we think of, but God's glory and we do him wrong by not providing a stone church in the parish of Midley."

I gave a nod in recognition of his understanding. "Can I see the plans?"

A cord was fastened around the prior's rotund waist, and from this a leather pouch, a bunch of keys and a knife hung. Tucked into the cord, a roll of vellum, held in place with a leather strap, nestled against his habit. Prior John released the roll and began to spread it over the ancient oak tabletop.

By now the morning sun had passed around the chancel end of the cathedral, but the table was placed under the barred windows to make the most of the light. Curious, I leaned forward to study the plans, ready to provide a lamp if needed.

The marks on the vellum were well-preserved, showing a rectangular nave and two aisles, all the same length. To the east, a square chancel protruded, and to the west a square tower. I leant forwards and squinted to read the measurements.

"The main body of the church is about sixty feet in length," I murmured. "A modest building, but with two aisles they will not lack space. How many priests does the village have?"

"Just the one," Prior John replied. "With forty-three adults living in the parish. Mostly farmers."

I knew little of village life, so concentrated on the sketches. The tower stood square and solid with a wooden spire. The windows were tall and elegant with flowing tracery, and buttresses supported the walls at regular intervals. "The ground can be soft," the prior informed me, pointing to the buttresses.

"I see our own designs reflected in this church," I said, noting the quatrefoil shape in the window tracery at the pointed tip of each window along the north and south walls.

"It is no surprise that Archbishop Sudbury wanted to recognise our own cathedral design when he decided on the details of this church."

"Ragstone?" I queried, thinking of the grey stone found in the North Downs.

"Aye, and timber from the land around Bilsington. Our friends at St Augustine's Priory can help with the arrangements for the wood."

I nodded. As steward, I had a broad knowledge of all our land and knew the hillside overlooking Romney Marsh to be wooded, but I had never been to the small priory and never expected to do so. My role at Christ Church filled all my time and although I had trusted assistants... My thoughts were interrupted:

"Brother Fabian, you are to go to Midley with a band of labourers to oversee the first stages of building the church and to negotiate the buying of stone and wood on the way."

*But I...* Thankfully, I managed to stop myself from uttering those words. I merely stuttered, "I am to... to leave Christ Church?"

"Someone must take charge of the money. You are still a young man, strong of body and mind. I need a trusted, senior monk to take the lead. The plans have been made, not only of the church, and detailed lists of the tools needed and labourers, skilled and unskilled, that will be required. Archbishop Sudbury worked with the former steward to estimate the costing. I will leave these with you." Prior John produced several small rolls of parchment and placed them on my table.

"And this is for next year?" I queried. "Next spring?"

"Next year!" he exclaimed. "Nay, we have the rest of summer and autumn ahead of us before the winter weather makes it hard to continue. You must train an assistant; I suggest Brother Michael is the most able and can be trusted with extra responsibility. Others will ensure the labourers, tools and equipment are ready."

"Ready for when?"

"Ten days is sufficient."

I have come to our chapel to find peace. My mind is in turmoil. I hold great responsibility here at Christ Church, accounting for the flow of coins in and out of the cathedral and priory. But my duties are carried out from my treasury room, or from within the walls of our holy buildings. Prior John is wrong – may God forgive me for thinking this – I have not the wisdom nor the experience to lead such a project.

# *Diggory*

Over ten days have passed since we heard of Archbishop Sudbury's death. His body came to Canterbury within days of the murder and has been buried in the quire of the cathedral. We, the common people of Canterbury, at first flocked into the parish churches to pray for the archbishop's soul. Later, we filed into the cathedral and knelt in silence before the burial chamber.

I wonder how it will be decorated and if, already, the cathedral masons are creating the carved stone sides of the tomb with an ornamental canopy. Will a figure of Simon Sudbury grace the slab?

From my place at West Gate, I fit the last pieces of the parapet and look down on those who enter the city. This morning a couple of monks, one of them the steward, came by and asked to speak with us.

"How long before the pilgrims come to visit our newly-murdered archbishop?" Mark had asked me earlier as we worked side by side.

I smiled, despite being shocked by my brother's words. "Do you think they will?"

12

"It all depends." Mark paused and, holding a length of straight wood, narrowed his eyes, assessing whether the course of stone was even. "Use the mallet on this one," he suggested. "To the right." Returning to my question, he continued, "It depends on whether there are miracles at the tomb. That's what brings the pilgrims."

"If there were to be, then it would be all for the good of Canterbury," I suggested.

We were not given the chance to explore this further as at that moment someone called up the stone staircase. "Westerns, are you there? Come on down, will you?"

"What's this about?" Mark said, largely to himself.

Having gathered our tools, we walked down the stairs to find our foreman, Thomas Stoneman, waiting with a pair of monks. "They're going about the place asking everyone…" he began.

We waited. Others came, including our father and uncle, cousins and neighbours. When about sixteen masons and half as many carpenters had gathered, Thomas told the monks, "This is most of them from West Gate and the wall along here. Those who are not with us will hear soon enough."

"Greetings, I am Brother Fabian, Steward at Christ Church Priory," the taller one introduced himself. "And this is Brother Michael."

"Greetings," we replied simultaneously, lowering our heads in a mark of respect.

"I need men, skilled and unskilled," Brother Fabian began. "A team of men – masons and carpenters."

*To work on the cathedral!* My thoughts ran away with themselves, and I stepped forward, raising my hand. "What can I do? Is it the nave?"

"Diggory Western," Thomas introduced me. "From a family of skilled masons. Not tied by a wife or children."

"Diggory!" Mark hissed at me. "What are you doing? What is it they want from us?"

"I thought..."

Brother Fabian stepped forward and spoke directly to me. "Wait and speak to me afterwards." Then he returned to his fellow monk and addressed us, "I need a team of men to come with me to a place called Midley on Romney Marsh where a new stone church will be built to replace an existing wooden one. We wish to fulfil all Archbishop Sudbury's visions for the diocese. We are to build a new church according to his plans!"

"Romney Marsh!" I heard Mark mutter. "Where on earth is *that*?"

"I'm not sure." I felt deflated. "Some place west of here, I think." I hardly dared hope that this new church would be built of Caen stone, giving me the opportunity to carve glorious decorative details. "It's not around here."

"Those who come with me will be paid handsomely. It means leaving Canterbury until the winter and returning to Midley again in the spring to complete the work. I need young, strong, healthy men who are prepared to leave their home and family."

"Will our work here in the city still be available on our return?" someone called out.

"There will be work for you on your return."

"If you have a wife and children who depend on you being here, or are responsible for the care of your parents, then this is not for you," Thomas Stoneman stated. "We can easily provide men from the many skilled craftsmen working here."

Most of the men drifted away, leaving just six of us. "So, Midley is a village? A village in this area you speak of called Romney Marsh?" Mark asked. He had stayed, despite having a wife and three young children to care for. He was curious, I assume.

"It is a small village between the old part of Romney and Lydd," Brother Fabian told us.

But these places meant nothing to us. Had he said Ramsgate or Dover or some place nearer to Canterbury, then we would have begun to understand.

"Does it have woodland, or coast or a river?" my uncle asked.

The monks considered this. "Nay. It is flat land, with fertile soil, drainage ditches and ancient creeks cutting through it."

"Well, I can't go, whatever the land is like," Mark responded. "I doubt any man in Canterbury would want to go to this place when we have work and homes here."

"Then you can go back to work, Mark Western, and those who are interested can report to the priory tomorrow," Thomas said, his tone stern. In his role as foreman, he was firm but fair, and he knew my brother would not consider working away from home. To the monks, he asked, "Where should my workers go to see you, if they are interested?"

"I will be at the Christ Church gate for the hour before noon tomorrow," Brother Fabian replied. "When I have half a dozen skilled masons, four carpenters and four to six unskilled men, then I will be satisfied. We will take lay monks to tend to our needs – our cooking and the washing of our clothes."

"The village of Midley is not large enough to offer us hospitality. We must fend for ourselves," Brother Michael added.

"Where will the men live?" Thomas asked.

"In barns, if possible, or in the wooden church." Brother Fabian shrugged. "There will be no lodging houses such as we have here." He bowed his head slightly. "I must move on. Thank you for your time and God bless you all."

As he walked past me, he paused and said, "We need men like you. Men who are keen to see new places and improve their skills. Men who would like a chance to have their decorative designs featured in wood and stone."

I hadn't voiced my thoughts aloud, not to the monk, but his words made me smile to myself. It seemed as if he knew me.

As my day working on West Gate came to an end, I heard Mark saying over and over that neither of us will be travelling across Kent to some remote place. It is different for him – he has a wife and children to think of. But I am free to do as I wish. Living with Mark and his wife, who is with child again, is not easy. We have such little space. My cot is narrow, and I must share with my younger brother, Paul. None of us has any room to call our own. If I could earn more, then perhaps I could have my own place, and maybe it could lead to better opportunities...

I have decided, although I will not speak to Mark about it yet, that I will go to see Brother Fabian tomorrow. Because maybe... just maybe... after the church is built, there will be a chance for me to join the cathedral masons.

# Brother
# Fabian

"Diggory Western and my brother, Paul."

I nodded. "May the Lord look kindly upon you."

As I approached, the brothers Western were already lingering at the gateway between the lay and the monk's cemeteries in the cathedral grounds. They waited patiently while a trestle table was set up and Brother Michael seated himself behind it, his ink and parchment spread out before him.

"Masons?" I asked.

"Aye," Diggory replied. I recognised him as the man who had shown enthusiasm yesterday before someone, his brother, I think, had cut him short.

"We've been working on West Gate," Paul told me, "but it's coming to an end."

"We are free to build this church at Midley," Diggory added. "And when we are back, there's the city wall to repair, all the way to North Gate."

There was no need to ask if these men were fit for the work. With clear skin, bright blue eyes and a stocky build, I could see they were both healthy and strong. As for their skills – I judged them to be over twenty years of age, but still youthful enough to embrace the task ahead of us. Diggory was most likely the oldest as he took the lead.

"Do you have people here depending on you?" I asked.

"Nay, we live with our brother and his family. Our parents live with our sister, her husband and children," Diggory responded.

"We are ready to see new places and are hard workers," Paul confirmed.

"You would be leaving within a week," Brother Michael told them. "Work must proceed with haste. It is not ideal to start such a project during the summer. The winter months will be biting at our heels. Spring would have been better."

"We understand and are ready." Diggory gave a confident smile. He was wasted as a mason – I imagined him standing in the cathedral quire with the light beaming upon his golden hair.

Brother Michael wrote 'masons' in his flowing script and their names underneath. "Meet us here next Friday morning at daybreak. Bring the tools of your trade, blankets, a flask of ale and food for your midday meal. Our pace will be slow, and if you want to carry your possessions by cart then it will not hinder us. Any questions?"

The brothers looked at each other.

"We'll earn more than we do here?" Paul asked, his tone hesitant.

"You will," Brother Michael responded. "And if I need to find you beforehand?"

"We'll be at West Gate," Diggory said. He turned to gaze at the cathedral nave – Sudbury's nave rising from the decaying Norman walls. The young mason murmured something, and I wanted to ask him if he aspired to work with the creamy Caen stone, but I had been in the priory too long – I didn't know how to make spontaneous conversation.

"Back to work then," Paul said to his brother. They glanced towards the gateway. A lone man strolled through.

"There's your first carpenter," Diggory remarked. "He's a good worker."

With that we said our farewells, the masons left, and we turned our attention to the next person who Brother Michael would add to our list.

# Gisella

## Romney Marsh

We are agog! Here at Midley we will talk of nothing else for days, most likely weeks. A messenger has come to see us. On the rare occasions that someone arrives with news, then they are just passing through and we happen to be on their route. Mostly they are lost, for there is no good reason for anyone to be travelling across this lonely land.

Yet this messenger, Rolf his name is, has ridden from Canterbury to speak to us. To speak to us!

I spotted him as I crouched amongst the rambling peas with the summer sun beating upon my back. My basket was already satisfyingly full of fresh pods, and I had just decided to return home. Movement from the direction of our church caused me to glance that way and I frowned, straining to focus on someone approaching by horse from the direction of the trackway, Kingsmarsh Lane. We only have workhorses here, short, sturdy, brown beasts. *Who could this be astride a sleek grey horse?*

Now standing to watch his progress, I wondered if I should hasten to tell my father. But, before the stranger had dismounted, the priest emerged from the church, and they were immediately engrossed in conversation. Then, with the horse being led on a loose rein, the priest indicated where my father was working in the field, and they set off together. Turning towards home, I raced along the lines of peas, eager to share the news with my mother.

From the peas, I passed onions, their bulbs just rising from the ground, and carrots with feathery tops. Then, dodging the chickens and a couple of feline mouse-catchers, I approached the back of our farmhouse.

Our home sits on the foundations of the first property built here at Midley. The stories of this land and the first settlers are passed down from one generation to the next. In those times Middle Isle, as they called it, was an island in the tidal River Rother, with the small town of Lydd being to the south-east and the old port of Romney on the riverbank to the north-east. The river at first silted up and later changed course, leaving its boggy bed and a mere trickle of water trailing though marshland. Middle Isle was no longer an isle.

This land became Midley, and my ancestors thrived here. They rebuilt the farmhouse and brought oxen to work the land. My father had the property reconstructed once more, and now it stands as a long, low, timber-framed home, its walls stuffed with mud, straw and stubble, its roof thatched with reed stalks. With our barns attached to one end, it is no wonder that our home is known as Longhouse Farm.

"There's a man! With a horse!" I called as I approached my mother. She was winding a bucket up from the well and barely turned towards me. "He's with the priest and going to speak to father now."

"What sort of man? A farmer from Romney way? A labourer looking for work? We don't need help, not with your brothers nearly full-grown men, but he could ask over Scotney way..."

I helped her pour the fresh water into jugs. "Not a labourer, nor someone looking for work," I replied. "He has a horse, not a cumbersome beast but a fine grey mare."

"We'll hear about it soon enough," Mother shrugged. "He'll be lost, wanting directions. Go and pull up some onions, will you? I wonder if the fish cart will come this way today or tomorrow."

Deflated, I left and returned to the vegetable plots. Having selected the onions, I cleaned out the chicken sheds and, as I piled straw and manure onto a heap, my father appeared with the stranger.

"Gisella," he called. "Where's your mother?"

"In the house," I replied, watching as the grey horse was tethered to a post.

Removing my apron, I followed, only pausing to dunk my hands in a barrel of water.

With the doors wide open to the front and back, we welcomed a tunnel of light through the home but that, and the pools of sunlight near the small windows, only made the shadowed corners even darker. The newcomer perched on a stool with a beaker of ale in his hand. He looked towards me. I found it was hard to make out his features with my eyes both adjusting to the dim interior and smarting from the woodsmoke.

"I've told Rolf, of course, that there is no village, least not what he'd expect," Father was saying. He paused. "Rolf this is my daughter, Gisella. Gisella, Rolf from Canterbury, come with news for us all." I nodded and murmured a brief greeting as my father continued, "So, I've asked Bernard to go about the place and tell everyone to gather by the church after their midday meal."

"He'll have to make haste," my mother observed.

"He's taken a pony," Father told her. "I've explained the lie of the land to Rolf."

He was referring to our church and its position within the parish. In the stories of Middle Isle, the first altar and cross were placed on the highest piece of land. Over the centuries this has become known as 'the nose' as it was not only slightly raised but stuck out, with its rounded end, into the river. The earth here remains thick with yellow sand, reminding us of the time when tidal waters flowed by. From the church in the north-east, Midley is a long parish with fertile soil and scattered cottages. Drained over the past century, it is much larger than the original island. If Rolf expected to find a cluster of cottages crowding around the church and alehouse, he would have been disappointed.

"He'll be halfway to Little Scotney by now," Father said, once more referring to my brother, Bernard. "Then he'll come back past Newland."

"How many in the parish?" Rolf from Canterbury asked.

"Forty-three adults, and by that, I mean over fourteen years of age. And children... perhaps twelve, perhaps more."

I was none the wiser as to what message Rolf had brought from Canterbury, and now the talk turned to accommodating him overnight. "Will you be staying in Midley?" Mother asked. "We can feed you, but as for a bed, the best we can offer is the loft in the barn." "I'd welcome a meal and some feed for my horse. Once she is rested, and I've spoken to the people of Midley, then I'll be on my way," he answered. "I've a bed in the new part of Romney for the night."

I loitered, still hoping to hear what news he brought, but Father had different ideas for me. "Gisella, make haste to Ned Smithy at Hawthorn

Corner and call on John Thatcher on the way. Tell them there's a parish meeting at the church and to come at noon."

"Aye, I'll do that." I left bearing news of the messenger from Canterbury, frustrated to have learned nothing about the reason for him being here.

"Thank you. Thank you for leaving your work to come and listen to me." Rolf from Canterbury stood on a crate provided by my father. He paused and his gaze roamed about our humble gathering.

"I bring news from Canterbury. Our archbishop has been murdered in London. Archbishop Sudbury is dead. God rest his soul."

I heard a sharp intake of breath... the murmurings of surprise, followed by horrified whispers. Everyone but the younger children recalled the archbishop's visit to Midley three years beforehand. Back then, news of his arrival had come ahead by messenger. He and his entourage had remained with us for a day, examining the church and land around it, and had left with scrolls of notes and sketches. I remember him being a bulky man with a thickset neck, but my observations were from a distance, and whether he was kindly or gruff I could not say.

More was to be revealed: "You will recall Archbishop Sudbury's visitation three summers ago," Rolf continued. "Plans were drawn up for a stone church to replace the wooden one. I have been sent to give you, the people of Midley, notice that a team of masons, carpenters and labourers have left Canterbury. Your stone church will be built in honour of our late archbishop."

Rolf of Canterbury paused, and questions immediately poured from the mouths of the assembled villagers:

"Where?"

"How big?"

"How will we feed and house the workers?"

"Will there be work for us?"

At the same time, they spoke to each other, adding to the hubbub:

"Listen to that – Midley has been noticed."

"What will it mean for us?"

"Men from Canterbury – will our daughters be safe?"

My father, reeve of Midley, stood beside the messenger and bellowed, "How can this good man answer your questions when you all chatter at once? The men will be housed in our wooden church and in my barns at Longhouse Farm, and wherever else there is room for them. They will bring with them a band of lay monks who will feed them and tend to their domestic needs. As for the church – there are plans and they will be left for us to view."

"What of my daughter and yours, Edwin?" Ned Smithy called.

"I trust they will be safe with the steward of Christ Church Priory supervising the venture," my father replied.

"I'm not speaking of the monks, although they are still men with men's desires..." This was followed by much sniggering. "I speak of the other men. Those building the church."

"All I can say is that those men have been chosen for their eagerness to build a church," Rolf told him. "They will have no more time to be chasing your daughters than any other man who comes to the village. But if there is trouble, then they will answer to Brother Fabian."

"We will welcome these men from Canterbury," my father stated. "We will welcome their news and stories of a place that few, if any, of us will ever visit. We will learn from their skills and give our thanks for a stone church." He turned to our priest, Father David.

"Safe journey for these men. The woodland on the far hills hides vagabonds, and the tracks across the marsh wind this way and that until travellers can make no sense of the place," the priest declared. "I pray for their safety."

"We will join you in your prayers," my father responded.

"You say they have left," the farmer from Newland questioned. "When can we expect them?"

We all turned to look in the direction of the old part of Romney, across the acres of land claimed from the wide riverbed.

"They left three days ago, the same as me," Rolf told us. "But whereas I ride unhindered, they come with cumbersome wagons. They are to stop at Lyminge and organise the buying of flint from the area, and then at Aldington to discuss acquiring worked blocks of ragstone* and at Bilsington to collect wood. The three wagons will be loaded as much as possible so building can start immediately."

"Their journey will be slow," my father concluded.

"A week or more," Rolf agreed. "The riverbed you speak of is dry and should remain so until the autumn. But there is a waterway cut through the land, and I fear the bridge is not strong enough to carry wagons with stone."

"We will prepare for their arrival to be in four days at the earliest," Father David decided. "And hope that the bridge across the Rhee is strong enough."

"Now we must wish you godspeed to Romney," Father announced, "and from there to Canterbury. You have spoken with me and our priest, and we will do our best to prepare everyone for the arrival."

As dusk falls upon Midley, settling over the Longhouse Farm and us – the ancestors of Edwin and Sarah Carpenter, the first to make the isle their permanent home – this news is all we can think of. Days have passed... months have passed... and no one has noticed our settlement. No news has come from any further than Lydd or Romney. Now there is news aplenty and much change to look forward to.


\* Author's note: Ragstone was not quarried at Aldington at this time. However, it suits my plot for it to be sourced from here.

# Gisella

Two days have passed since the messenger came. As I work on the land or walk from one place to another, I keep an eye on the track coming from the east. One day soon I will look, and they will appear – the men and their wagons on the track to Midley. We are all waiting. All scanning our surroundings for a glimpse of the new arrivals.

These last few days have been busy. My father has met several times with Father David and local farmers. Longhouse is the nearest property to the church, other than the priest's small cottage, and my parents say that six men can bed down in the barn loft. Newland Farm can offer accommodation for four, but Little Scotney lies at the far end of the parish and some distance from where they will be building the church. So, my father has been to Swamp Farm, in the neighbouring parish but as close to our church as Longhouse, and the farmer has agreed to allow four to stay there. The monks will sleep in our wooden church.

"I asked Father David where Brother Fabian, the steward, will sleep," Mother told us as we sat at a table outside our home with bowls of broth and chunks of bread to dip. "He is a quire monk – not the same as being a lay monk. They live separately in the priory."

"The chancel?" I asked. "There's a screen..."

"We decided, or at least Father David decided, that he can share his home," Mother said. "He will give up his bedchamber and claims the loft above the stable will be comfortable enough."

I tried to imagine the monks' world – their home beside the huge cathedral, surrounded by the city. We occasionally meet someone who has travelled to Canterbury, but to picture the towering holy place, city walls and gateways is near impossible. Lydd has a huge church, but the stonework is plain and not comparable. The new part of Romney, however, does boast a church with decorative carving. I have seen it twice and each time I squint and crane my neck to look at the carved faces on the tower, some of them at the very top surrounding the stone spire. 'It is like the cathedral', someone once said to me. 'But the cathedral is more, so much more of everything.'

This evening, before dusk fell upon our land, I wandered along to the sandy rise and stood gazing at our wooden church. The air smelt sweet and was thick with summer pollen. Insects hummed and hovered over the winding waterway. Knowing that, within days, Midley would be changed forever, I felt drawn to our holy building and wanted to absorb every detail. Upright planks met with a row of small, high windows which, in turn, met the thatched roof. To the west, a small, open porch led to a pair of carved doors, but I chose not to enter. Instead, I meandered towards the chancel end where a single lancet window had been fitted. Through the thick glass I saw the faint glow of the sanctuary lamp. I wondered if we had, unknowingly, attended our last service here. Will our priest ask that the altar be moved and a temporary shelter made for it, or will the men lodging in the church clear away their pallets, mattresses and blankets so we can continue to worship here?

So many changes for our humble settlement. I welcome them mostly and occasionally fear them.

# *Diggory*

Today I saw Romney Marsh for the first time. We craftsmen and labourers stood on the hillside in the grounds of a holy place called St Augustine's Priory, near the village of Bilsington, and scanned the flat land spread out before us.

"Where's Midley?" someone asked.

"I don't know," replied the lad from a local farm who had come to take us to our lodgings. "There's Newchurch down yonder, and Eastbridge, but Midley... It's not local to here, I can tell you that much."

"But it's there somewhere. There on Romney Marsh."

"It must be one of those small places that no one talks about," the lad conceded. "This summer sun plays tricks on us. It's all a haze. Come at first light and everything will be sharp. If Midley can be seen, you'll see it then. Someone will know where it is."

"Will we reach it tomorrow?" my brother Paul asked.

"Not with three lumbering wagons if it's way over the other side." He shrugged.

"And what's it like on Romney Marsh?" I asked. "What sort of people live there? What do they do?"

"They're farmers," he told us. "Farmers and ditch clearers and, if they live near the coast, then they fish. It's a place with rich soil, but those who own that good soil, they live up here on the hills."

"Why's that?"

"Bad air," he said. "You won't all come back. I can tell you that much about the Marsh."

Exhausted after five days of travelling, we turned away from the view and looked at each other, calculating who might be the weakest. Every one of us has been chosen for his health, youth and strength – could it be true that some would not return?

"Let's get you settled in the barns," the lad suggested.

Our walk has been short today, but the work beforehand was strenuous. Having arrived at Aldington late yesterday evening, the first hours of this morning were spent waiting for Brother Fabian to negotiate the buying of ragstone blocks. Then all hands were set to loading one of our wagons, followed by loading two belonging to the quarry. These will depart for Midley a couple of days after us. After that, the walk to Bilsington took no time at all, but now Brother Fabian is discussing the buying of wood from the priory lands. When we leave here, all three of our carts will be loaded, the first being laden with flint from Lyminge, as well as carrying our own belongings.

"When it is all agreed, you will load the last cart," he told us. Our respite will be brief.

Yesterday I noticed that Brother Fabian keeps a fat purse nestled in the folds of his tunic. I haven't mentioned it to anyone else because I imagine it contains a fortune in coins – enough to build a stone church, or at least enough to start the construction. There is also a small chest which is always guarded by two lay monks. I wonder if this chest contains the coins needed to pay us workers and for food and lodgings on the way, while the purse holds gold to pay for the materials we need. Perhaps it holds nothing more than his rosary beads and book of hours, but I like to picture it is stuffed with delicate gold nobles, the most valuable coin in this kingdom.

# Brother Fabian

Flint. Stone. Wood. Already my purse is a little lighter. This morning, we left St Augustine's behind us and walked first to Bilsington village, then down the hill to Romney Marsh. It is not the first hill we have negotiated but is the first with three wagons loaded to full capacity. We removed half the supplies from each cart, leaving them at the roadside guarded by two men. Then, glad of a new design in shafts which keeps the horses safe, inch by inch and one cart at a time, we descended the steep hillside, with us all crowded around the back and sides, ready to restrain it. Having left Bilsington at dawn, the morning was well underway by the time we were all safely on the low land which is Romney Marsh.

The sun shone in a cloudless sky and from near-empty ditches stagnant water belched its foul odour. Insects hovered and the horizon shimmered. To negotiate the Marsh in the rain would be dismal, but to journey here in the height of summer brings its own difficulties.

We came across Newchurch easily enough, for the track took us directly to that small village. The people made us welcome, offering cool ale, and suggesting that we sit for a while in the shade of the church walls. The masons circled the building taking in the decorative details.

The priest wanted to give me a personal tour. "St Peter and St Paul," he said, pointing to the bearded faces at the end of the hood moulds over the tower doorway.

"Worthy saints," I murmured. Privately, I thought their carved eyes looked sad and their features lacked precision. I am spoilt by the images at Canterbury. *God forgive me for my pride.*

From Newchurch we trudged along mile after mile of winding lanes. I am a man of books, unused to such exercise, and exhaustion soon came upon me. It wrapped itself around me, pressing upon my forehead, burning my eyes and making my limbs heavy. One of the lay monks, Brother Francis, took the map from me. "I know this place a little," he said. "I'll lead the way if you prefer." So, I followed, placing one foot before the other, losing all sense of my surroundings. In time, we neared the village of Ivychurch.

"Brother Fabian, your skin is burning," Brother Francis remarked. "Would you care to sit in the shade of this willow tree, and I will speak with the people here? Hopefully there is accommodation for us in this church, and someone who can offer you a remedy to calm the fever."

Not long after, I was helped to a cool corner of the church where someone had kindly provided a pallet and a mattress for me to sleep on. They seemed to expect nothing from me, and I was grateful. I took off my shoes and felt for my pouch filled with gold nobles, but instead of wrapping my hand around a plump bag, my fingers touched upon some coins and loose folds of material. I felt around my tunic and pulled three coins from the woollen cloth. *It is the fever. You are imagining things which are not the truth.* Instead, I pictured the pouch, rounded and heavy in my palm, and me placing it against my body so it lay snug while I slept. Then someone, perhaps a wise woman from the village, gave me a herbal draft and I slept a deep, dreamless sleep.

# Diggory

Our journey is almost over. Today we arrived in a place called Ivychurch and tomorrow we will be in Midley. Let me tell you about Ivychurch. It is a village with very few houses and a church large enough to serve a city! I have spotted a forge, a beerhouse and a bakehouse. A thatcher and a carpenter complete the local trades. Cottages are scattered, and not more than a dozen of them, although there will be several farms within the parish.

The people of Ivychurch welcomed us but their attention immediately fell upon the steward, with his dazed expression and sweat glistening on his glowing brow. With help from a couple of lay monks, Brother Fabian was provided with a place to rest in a quiet corner, and we heard he had soon settled into a deep sleep.

Now left with no leader for our band of workers, it was Paul and I who explained to the reeve and priest our reason for passing through. Brother Francis spoke of the route we were to take to Midley. We were told that the church could accommodate us all overnight, leaving Brother Fabian in his own hastily curtained cell set apart from the rest of us. This would be the first night spent with the lay monks and labourers under the same roof. Until now the monks had slept in a religious house or church, while we stayed in a barn or loft.

Once all this was settled, we sat on roughly hewn benches on a narrow patch of land between alehouse and graveyard. With clay beakers in our hands and our backs to the alehouse, we could focus on the vast church.

"It has been extended over the past decades." The reeve gestured towards the church. "Two aisles, both as long as the nave and chancel combined. They contain chapels, of course, and we have a chantry priest as well as our priest. He keeps the light of St Katherine burning on her altar."

"Is there more to your village?" I asked. "Who fills this church?"

"Ivychurch is no more than these properties and the farms," I was told, "although the parish stretches all the way to the Sussex border, some six miles away."

"You've suffered badly from the black death?" Harry Woodman, a master carpenter, suggested. "This church was planned when the village was bigger? Much bigger?"

"We have suffered, but no more than anywhere else. This land belongs to Christ Church Priory, and it is they who decided on the size." The reeve glanced towards the church and continued, "I trust that Canterbury will help maintain it."

An uneasy silence fell upon our small group, then the reeve continued, "Come, we can view the church without disturbing your steward. We have a dozen men working on it, masons and carpenters like yourselves. Speak with them. You may learn something about the ground you'll be building on."

With some reluctance, as it was pleasant to sit in the shade of the alehouse idly watching the village masons and carpenters at work, we rose and began to amble around the outer walls where sturdy buttresses were being constructed. A mason explained that water was never far from the surface of this land. "When you build your church, do not skimp on supporting it," we were told. "There's not a church on the Marsh where the columns do not lean outwards, despite our best efforts."

"And after the buttresses are complete?" we asked.

"A porch. With a room above for visiting priests."

I thought of Brother Fabian sleeping in a corner of the church.

We reached the east end and from here the tower of St Mary's could be seen, a church we had passed at a distance just a short time before reaching Ivychurch.

"Will you have a tower?" I asked. It seemed odd for this edifice to be so long and so wide, yet to have no tower.

"In time..." they replied. "First we are to build a turret to allow access to the roof once the scaffold is removed."

"This church will not be completed in my lifetime," one of the masons reflected. "Nor that of my sons."

With this, I am sure that every mason and carpenter in our team from Canterbury wondered how long our own church at Midley would take to construct. The plans showed it to be modest, but would they change? *Nay*, I decided. *This parish of Ivychurch is large, whereas Midley is no more than a slither of land between larger and richer parishes.*

We peeped inside the church, staggered by the cavernous space. Even with oak screens separating the far end, providing the priests their own private space at the altar, the area for the village people felt huge. My gaze focussed on the flicker of the burning candle within the sanctuary lamp, suspended from the ceiling by a long chain and partially obscured by the rood screen. Then I studied the simple wall paintings in the form of lines to represent blocks of stone, rambling vines and symbolic flowers. The more detailed artwork lay behind the screens and, like the lamps, I could only see a hint of them. On my way out, I spotted four columns of stone from Caen.

My thoughts returned to Canterbury and our golden cathedral. If I proved myself at Midley, was there a chance of my being accepted onto the team of master masons who worked with this stone all day long? Might a very small amount of Caen stone be used in our new church? Might I be able to carve a decorative feature – perhaps a face?

"Come on, Diggory," Paul murmured. "We must settle the horses and eat."

# Brother Fabian

Something terrible has happened. I wish I had remained at Christ Church. With my coffers and my ledgers, I lived according to the Rule of St Benedict and could be trusted to do right. Now I have left the priory and lost direction. First the fever came, making me unfit to lead the men, and now the coins have gone.

I woke, not long ago, to find myself in a curtained corner of what appeared to be a huge church. Not a grand church, because it lacks the sculptural details which we from Canterbury are so used to, but a great barn of a building. At first unsure if it was the same day or the next, I studied the light and saw that it blazed through the eastern windows. I listened and heard a chisel chipping upon stone and a saw cutting into wood. *Dawn has passed and men are at work somewhere nearby. What men?*

Easing myself up, I swung around so I sat on the edge of a pallet. *Wherever I am, people have been good to me.* Reaching for a beaker, I took a sip. It tasted of herbs and cleansed my dry mouth. I touched my forehead. It felt cool. "Thank you, Lord. You have spared me."

*I must get up. Find my men.* Reaching for my shoes, I slipped one foot and then the other into the soft leather and pulled on the laces. *Will they have left without me?* My sense of peace left me. Taking a slow, deep breath, I whispered to myself, "The men are here waiting for you."

*What is this?* A sliver of something hard clung to the woollen skirt of my tunic. As I pulled it off, my fingers brushed against more smooth metal. The coins, having relinquished their grip on the material, settled in my palm, both turned so a jubilant King Edward, sword in hand, faced me. *My nobles. My gold nobles.*

Panic took hold and, still sitting, I began a frantic search for the gold. My hand flew to my waist where the pouch hung open, a few coins still nestled in its folds. Three more lay together on the blanket covering the straw mattress. One sat snug in the hem of my tunic. I stood and two fell to the ground. "Twelve. Twelve coins!"

*How many did I start with? Thirty. One used for flint. Two for wood. Three for stone. How many should I have? Twenty-four.*

Standing, I shook out the blankets, lifted the mattress and examined my tunic once more. No more gold nobles revealed themselves.

# *Diggory*

Our leader, Brother Fabian, has left Ivychurch. Not for Midley but to retrace his steps to Newchurch. At first, I thought that the fever had allowed the devil to possess our good monk as, shortly after dawn, I saw him crawling along the village road. His hands searched the ground as he moved, and his tunic trailed in the dust.

Not long after that, Brother Francis called a meeting. "Bad news," he stated without drama. "Our steward, Brother Fabian, was carrying a pouch of gold nobles. The clasp has broken, and the contents spilt."

"How many?" Paul asked.

"How many lost?" the monk replied. "I'm not sure. Some remained in the folds of material, some clung to the fabric of his tunic, a few had been used to pay for the flint, stone and timber. I could get no sense from him and we, the lay monks, were not privy to the amount he carried. Perhaps ten, perhaps fifteen nobles are gone."

Silence fell upon our group. Not one of us could imagine the value of those coins. As workers we dealt in pennies and grouts. The lay monks had no money or possessions.

"And his fever?" I wondered.

"The fever and sweats have passed, but he has such a panic running through him that I fear for his reasoning," Brother Francis admitted.

"These coins..." one of the carpenters began, "they were for building the church?"

"Aye, for the materials. We have a chest of smaller coins, but Brother Fabian always kept the nobles with him."

Over the days we had trekked from Canterbury to Romney Marsh, the relationship between us masons, carpenters, labourers and the four lay monks had become one of mutual respect. After all, these monks were workers too and they came from humble backgrounds. With Brother Fabian they still followed the Rule of St Benedict, often whispering the words of the psalms and daily prayers while going about their tasks. The rest of us began to recognise the pattern to their days and we kept our talk to a minimum during their times of prayer. Holding a senior position within the priory, Brother Fabian was as distant from the lay brothers as he was from the rest of us. He tended to walk alone, seeming to be deep in thought, and sometimes I wondered if he felt burdened by his responsibilities. The lay monks seemed to know about life beyond the cathedral and priory, but what did Brother Fabian know of how the laity lived and worked?

"What shall we do?" I asked. "Brother Francis, you led us here to Ivychurch, and we need someone to make decisions. In a band of nearly twenty men someone has to lead, and you know this land."

"I do," Brother Francis replied. "I come from a small village named after its church, St Marys. It's not far from here; we passed within a mile. But it is not for me to lead."

"Someone has to as none of us knows the way to Midley and it seems that, even if the sickness has passed from the steward's body, it lingers in his mind," another of the carpenters said.

"My brother Diggory was the first to join this mission," Paul began. "Let him represent the masons. Harry, you can represent the carpenters and you, Brother Francis, the monks. Together you will decide what we must do."

We three looked at each other and nodded. "Very well," Brother Francis agreed. "I suggest that we monks and some of you help Brother Fabian search for the lost coins, retracing our steps back to Newchurch if necessary."

"Diggory and I can speak to the priest and the reeve," Harry continued. "We may need to stay here for another night and could offer our labour in return for their hospitality?"

"Good idea," I agreed. "Who knows how many times we may pass through Ivychurch over the coming months. It would be no hardship to make friends with these good people."

By now some of the village masons and carpenters were emerging from their homes and lodgings. Harry and I approached them and soon an arrangement was made. Eight of us would labour with them while the rest would follow in the path of Brother Fabian. They said the priest would be along shortly and the reeve was an easy-going fellow who would not fuss over us lingering in Ivychurch.

We worked all morning under their guidance: the carpenters helping to take apart and rebuild a scaffold, while the masons constructed buttresses on the south-eastern corner of the church. I enjoyed the work and the opportunity to learn more about this place they called 'The Marsh' despite there being no sign of any boggy land.

"No sign of it," they agreed. "But there's a reason for these buttresses."

We had all spotted waterways winding this way and that. Although we hadn't yet learnt the ways of the Marsh, we believed these to be drainage ditches and without them the land would indeed be marsh.

"Over here, this side of the Rhee, it's all like this – fine farming land," one of the Ivychurch masons told me. "But over there – over at Midley where you're going – there's great banks of earth and they try to keep the sea at bay, but sometimes it breaks through. One moment it's farmland and the next moment it's marsh again."

"The Rhee?" I queried. "What's that? Another village?"

"Nay! It's a waterway. Made by man. Takes water from inland and they try to use it to flush out the old harbour, down at Romney. The new part of Romney."

"Oh, I see." But I didn't.

"You'll have to cross it. There's a strong bridge at the old part of Romney but I'd be unloading those wagons first."

It sounded like trouble, but Brother Fabian had directions and no doubt it was all part of the plan. However, marshland at Midley – this disturbed me.

"Why are we building a church where the sea could still break through?" I wondered.

"There's the isle and then there's the rest of it," a mason explained. "The isle, or what was an island, is higher ground. Only a bit, but it's enough. Then the rest of the land has been drained and farmed since the great storm."

We had been told about the 13th century storms when we stopped at Bilsington.

As we worked, those of us from Canterbury tried not to speak about the lost coins or the reason for staying in Ivychurch. A feeling of embarrassment and shame hung over us, despite none of us knowing about the gold until this morning. But when the new scaffold stood steady, we were given the chance to view Romney Marsh from the church roof. We could see for miles and were surprised to spot so many churches, yet so few cottages. All Saints, St Clement, St Mary the Virgin, St Peter and St Paul, St Dunstan – all so close. And further away the sturdy tower of St Nicholas and the slimmer, taller tower of another dedicated to All Saints.

"One day we'll come back here and see another tower," I said. "Our tower at Midley."

# Brother Fabian

I know God has not created me to be a leader of men. He made me a solitary fellow who can count money, log it and allocate it fairly. The coins have gone. Vanished. Taken by the Marsh.

We searched the tracks and verges, the places where we had sat and rested, but the gold could not be found. Not once was there a glint of soft yellow – a hint of a partly hidden coin.

I left Canterbury with thirty nobles and twelve are lost. Just to think of it causes my skin to burn and a sweat to break out. I wish the fever had taken me in the night. But that is not His plan for me. What does He want of me?

In my absence, the other men chose a group of three to lead them. These three are Brother Francis, who knows this land and led us to Ivychurch when my mind and body failed me; Diggory Western, the mason and first to put his name down to join me in the task of building a new church; Harry Woodman, the carpenter who was so helpful when we selected the timber needed from the woodland at Bilsington.

I have asked these good men to continue to help me lead the men. They agreed readily. If I had been forced to beg them then I would have done so.

Dusk has not yet fallen upon Ivychurch. The men who remained here have laboured all day building buttresses and securing scaffolding. Now they are being fed by the villagers and will make merry at the alehouse until nightfall. As for myself, I am exhausted. My whole being is heavy and my head throbs. I am lying on my pallet in my curtained corner of this cavernous church and all I can do is pray for guidance over the coming days.

# Gisella

## Midley

This afternoon the men from Canterbury arrived! At times I've wondered if their plans have changed, and we are to be left with our wooden church. But now they are here! There are two brothers, Diggory and Paul Western, both with fine upright figures, golden hair and ready smiles. I have learnt that they are masons, whereas some of their companions are carpenters, some unskilled workers and others are monks. What a collection of men to have in our village! Not that the monks count, but they look friendly enough. The masons are the most important of them all, at least that is my opinion. The church is to be made of stone, and they will be the ones to build it. And of all the masons, Diggory seems to be their leader. He is part of a small group who spoke with my father not long after their arrival.

There is one monk who is meant to be the leader of all these men. He is the one in charge. Yet, he appears to be the least fit of them all. When they arrived, amongst all the talk, I heard that this monk, Brother Fabian, is steward at the priory in Canterbury. My brothers and I were unsure of what a steward did, but in time we realised that he oversaw the money. We have only seen him once, as he is a private man who wishes to hide away in the chancel of our church.

They reached us by track from Swamp Road, and my whole family went to greet them with Father David. I felt overwhelmed – we have never had such a crowd come to Midley. Not only were there the men, but three wagons and six heavy horses. Some men immediately set about caring for these beasts, while others gathered around our priest and my father.

"Edwin Midisle is reeve here," Father David said as he introduced my father. "He descends from the first settlers and lives over there at Longhouse Farm, the closest property to the church. Six of you can sleep in the barn loft. The next closest property is Swamp Farm, although not in this parish; they will take four of you."

"And the others?" a lay monk asked. He had introduced himself as Brother Francis and said his family lived not far away in a village named St Marys, after the church.

"They can stay in farms which are a little further away," my father answered. "The wooden church will be for you monks."

"Brother Fabian, you can stay with me," Father David said, nodding towards his humble home near our church.

"Thank you," the steward replied.

"We have formed a small group of leaders," Brother Francis told us. "Brother Fabian has been ill since our arrival at Ivychurch, and we could not expect him to guide us across this land which is foreign to us."

That explained why their leader seemed unfit to lead. My mother and I exchanged glances, and I knew what she thought: *Please God, do not bring the plague to us.*

He must have read our thoughts, for Brother Francis swiftly added, "But he is feeling better already. The walking has wearied him though..."

We murmured our sympathies.

"Juliana... Gisella, can we feed our guests?" Father asked.

For the last few days, mother and I had been ready to offer a meal of thick broth with chunks of bread when the men from Canterbury arrived. Now we had to work quickly to prepare the vegetables and have them simmering in a pan with pork and barley.

"Will you join us for a meal at Longhouse?" my mother offered. "It will be informal as we are unused to having so many newcomers to Midley, but you are welcome to share our simple fare."

"Thank you," Brother Francis replied. "We monks are here to prepare meals for those building the church but are, as yet, unprepared."

"Then my daughter and I will welcome you all to our hearth before evening sets in. We cook and eat outside when the weather allows us to and cannot offer a comfortable seat for you all, but will do our best to offer hospitality."

"Bernard or Eliot can bring the masons over before that," my father suggested. "Make use of my sons if you need help unloading your wagons or carrying your belongings to the farms. Our land and beasts can spare us for the afternoon."

Mother and I left the men, although I think we were both reluctant, wanting to know more of their plans. My brothers would be in the heart of it, getting to know these people, whereas we women would have to wait until they gathered to eat.

"By then they will be settled, each one knowing where they will sleep over the coming months. This afternoon, all they will do is unload and carry and get to know the lie of the land," Mother said when I voiced my frustrations. "When they sit around our hearth, with a bowl of broth and a beaker of ale, they'll relax and that's when we'll learn about them."

"Is there is a story to be told about the steward?" I wondered as I carried a bowl of onions, turnips and carrots from our store on the cool, northern side of our home. We were preparing the meal outside, on the trestle table which saw so much activity during the warmer months of the year. "They say he is ill, but there is something else..."

"He is just weary. The other men are labourers, whereas Brother Fabian works at his desk." Mother placed pork fat in our largest pan before carrying it to the fire which smouldered within an earth pit. She lifted a kettle from the trivet, setting it on the dry earth, and replaced it with the pan.

"I cannot help but wonder why he had so little to say," I persisted as I peeled crisp golden skins off the onions. "Who is the other monk? Why does he seem to lead them?"

"Brother Fabian, the steward, holds an important role within the priory," my mother reminded me. "He is a quire monk, a monk who has taken holy orders. The others are the lay monks who will feed the workers and take care of domestic duties. If Brother Francis leads, it is only because he knows Romney Marsh."

"I cannot wait to hear more about them." We continued to chat idly as she seared the meat. I chopped vegetables to add to the pan, and Mother tipped in barley and water. By the time the masons came to see our barn loft, I was gathering herbs from

60

the plot not far from the house, and my mother had gathered as many plates and bowls as she could find.

Sometimes I think of the stone church that will soon rise on the sandy knoll beside our wooden church, but mostly I think of all the things to be learned about life beyond Romney Marsh. Our population has swelled. From here to Newland Farm, every dry loft or spare corner of a barn is filled with rolls of bedding and sacks. *What have they brought with them from Canterbury?* Spare tunics, stockings, shifts and precious mementos from their home, I imagine. I would like to know... I would like to know exactly what they have. The craftsmen also store their own tools with their personal belongings. They must take these tools of their trade from one place of work to the next.

Now the masons are making their home in our barn loft, and I hope they approve of our humble offering to them.

"Juliana," my father called to my mother just now. "Do you have an old cloth – a blanket perhaps? Bernard and I are to set up a screen behind the barn."

Mother looked at me and frowned.

"He wants to make them a place to wash? A private place?" I suggested.

"Gisella will fetch something," she answered. Then to me, "Gisella, go to the basket at the bottom of my bed. There's a sheet of rough hemp in there. That will do."

I race off, away from the simmering broth and the plates of flatbreads, through the main room of our home, barely faltering despite the dim light within. At the basket I pause, my fingers searching amongst the wool, the linen and – here it is! – the hemp. Then out again, this time rounding the end of Longhouse as I run towards the barn. My curiosity has no bounds. Here is my chance to get a little nearer and perhaps peep into the lives of these men from Canterbury.

# Gisella

The day started with the masons leaving Longhouse Farm not long after daybreak.

"Come back and join us when we break our fast?" my mother offered. "You are welcome."

"You've been very generous," Diggory replied, "but we came with plenty of food and the monks will feed us."

"If you need anything…"

"Then I'll tell Brother Francis. We mustn't take food you'll be needing to store for the winter months. I believe they plan to grow some vegetables, but also to travel to the larger towns to buy produce."

"We cannot expect Midley to provide for us," Paul added.

"We will do what we can," my mother insisted.

Not long after that, as I was tending the chickens and goats, I saw a thin trail of smoke spiralling upwards. *Brother Francis and the lay monks have made a fire! They said that they can feed themselves, and I can see they are determined to do so.*

By the time we were eating our breakfast, my brother Bernard had already been to cut wood for the priest as he does a couple of times a week. "They have put pegs in the ground and are fixing strings," he told us. "I saw where the new church will be!"

From our land, we watch as local people crowd about the site for the stone church. There are Midley people who only venture to our end of the parish to go to church, to see the blacksmith or carpenter, or for some other business. Yet today they come and seemingly for no reason but to see the newcomers for themselves. Even the farmer from Cheyne Court rode over with some talk of looking for the thatcher yet left without seeing him.

Everyone wants to know what these men are like. What skills do they have? Are they friendly? They want to know exactly where the church will be built and how long it will take to build it.

It is a day where we go about our usual tasks, but always with an eye on what the Canterbury men are doing. Already, our family has a special interest in the masons because they are living with us, and we will get to know them better than the others. Our conversation is no longer about if the wheat is ripening, how many eggs have been collected or if the strawberries have finished cropping. We only speak about the masons: are they comfortable, do they have everything they need, do they miss their families? We wonder about the others: what brought them to Midley, are they being made welcome at Newland and Swamp Farms?

Before, we had to travel to Lydd or Romney to have our minds filled with new sights and curiosities. Now there is so much to learn right here in Midley. I am fascinated by these people and the lives they lead in the city.

# Diggory

Today, on my first working day at Midley, I am glad I left Canterbury for this new land. Perhaps, as the weeks pass, it will seem like a lonely place. For now, it is all new to me and there are still so many places to explore. Besides, there is a church to build from the foundations upwards. Whereas before I patched, repaired and rebuilt, now we work from the very beginning.

The good folk from Longhouse are welcoming and, although they have little to give, they are generous. Bernard and Eliot, who are at the age where they are a curious mixture of man and boy, were willing helpers yesterday while we settled both ourselves and the horses. Their father, Edwin, took charge from the beginning, ensuring everyone had shelter for the night and making us feel welcome. Their mother, Juliana, fed us, and a merry affair that was, sitting on benches or on the parched grass until the last of the sun's rays left the sky. Not only have we newcomers all become friends, but we know we will live and work here with the blessing of the Midley folk.

The lay monks are friendly fellows, and it is only Brother Fabian who keeps apart from the rest of us. I believe he will always remain on the outside of our group; he is, by nature, a solitary man. As well as this, his position as steward at Christ Church Priory keeps him apart from us labourers and even the lay monks. Last night he remained at the priest's house, resting after his sickness and the long trek to Midley. The priest, Father David, joined us all for supper, and reported that Brother Fabian wanted no more than dry bread to eat and to be left in peace with his prayers.

"I have only seen him briefly," Juliana of Longhouse said to me yesterday when I went to thank her for the meal, "but I fear Brother Fabian is troubled."

"He is exhausted," I reminded her. "Whereas the rest of us are used to labouring all day, he…" I paused, unsure of what the steward does.

"He prays and counts money?" she suggested. Then she shrugged, "What do I know of life in a cathedral?"

We, the men from Canterbury, have not yet told the people of Midley about the lost nobles. We decided to wait and see how they accepted us and, more importantly, for our steward's health to recover.

There is a fifth member of Edwin and Juliana's family. Gisella is older than Bernard by a year or two.

She works with her mother, running the home and tending the small patches of herbs and vegetables close to Longhouse. As we work, plotting where the walls of the church will stand, I can see her slim body and the sway of her long nut-brown hair in the distance. The moment I saw Gisella, I noted that her hair hung uncovered, meaning that she is, as yet, unmarried. Perhaps she has a young man, and they have plans to marry. Perhaps, as I move the pegs and strings an inch or so this way, a foot that way, there is a man preparing a home for her to live in as his bride. If he is, then I have seen no sign of him. Often my thoughts return to Gisella – her interest in our building plans and our lives at home in Canterbury. I think of her merry smile, her lively manner and how, when I speak to her, she looks at me and answers with confidence. Yesterday, Gisella worked alongside Juliana to provide a hearty meal for us newcomers and I made sure that I thanked them both.

I think of her a lot, but I know when she sees me her thoughts do not stray to a possible romance. Paul, who is to marry when he returns to Canterbury in the autumn, has told me that young women stutter and blush if they are attracted to you. Gisella merely smiles and speaks with ease.

Enough of this foolishness. I am here to build a church.

The new holy place is to stand beside the old one. There is a slight rise in the land and the earth is surprisingly sandy – a rich, golden sand. I am told this harks back to the days when Midley was an island. Archbishop Sudbury had already decided where he wanted the stone church to be built, on the northern side of the wooden one.

"We are on the tip of Middle Isle," Brother Francis said as he surveyed the rectangle of the nave marked out with string. Harry Woodman and I stood either side of him. "See how the land drops away here. And all this was river. All the way over to Romney."

We had already learnt about that when we cautiously crossed the Rhee with a reduced load in our wagons, and then a stretch of lower land, with fresh cuttings for water to drain into.

"We are on the very edge of the parish boundary," he said. "As close to Canterbury as we can be while still in Midley." Then he asked me, "Is this sixty feet in length?"

"Aye. The same as the plan."

"It is too soon to talk about it with Brother Fabian, but let's make the nave fifty feet long. How is the stone to be paid for when so many nobles have been lost? If they are found no one will notice; if they are not found we need to save money where we can. Mark out forty-eight feet for the nave, another twelve for the chancel, and start on the foundations for them. Sixty altogether."

"And the aisles?" I asked.

"They can be added later. Will anyone query if we dig and build the foundations for the nave and chancel before the aisles?"

Harry and I looked at each other and together we replied, "Nay. At least not at first."

"And the tower?" Harry asked.

"Allow for a small bell tower. Enough to hold one bell."

"This way we can start work without delay," I said, "and when Brother Fabian is fully recovered, he can tell us what he wants us to do. Perhaps he will return to Canterbury for more gold, or perhaps the gold will be found?"

"When Brother Fabian recovers?" Harry muttered. "His body may recover, but I fear for his mind."

"Twelve feet off the length then." I ignored Harry's words while secretly agreeing with him. "And no aisles, but we'll have a small tower."

If I were to stop and thank God for something, then I would thank him for allowing us to have Brother Francis with us. He understands this land and is well-liked by both the skilled craftsmen, labourers and monks. While he mostly leaves Harry and me to measure and plan for the foundations, the monk is overseeing the domestic side to our living here. Yesterday all foodstuffs and cooking utensils were unloaded and now line the back wall of the wooden church, with the food placed on a line of hastily constructed shelves. On the floor there are pans, crates of plates and beakers, and barrels of weak ale alongside flagons of wine. Outside, a pit has been dug for a fire, but this place is so bare of trees that the lay monks are reluctant to take wood from those who live nearby. I have already spotted Bernard cutting wood for the priest, so perhaps there is an arrangement that he has wood supplied by those who live at Longhouse.

*How long will it last?* I found myself wondering as I saw a monk carrying a basket of food from the store in the church. He settled down to prepare it, while another stoked the fire.

My questions were answered by mid-morning when we supped ale and ate hard biscuits, both of which had travelled with us from Canterbury. Two of the lay monks were absent and I asked Brother Francis where they were.

"Young Eliot has taken them to some place near Lydd where they hope to be able to find someone to supply us with wood."

"Is there much wood there?" I asked, gazing across the flat land to a cluster of cottages and a stately church tower. In the heat of the summer day, the town looked distant, and I couldn't see any woodland.

"I hear there's holly trees growing on the shingle to the south-west of the town. They use the wood for sea defences, but there must be spare – the branches and offcuts."

The evening before we had heard about the mass of shingle stretching inland from the coast, but with trees growing on it – now that came as a surprise.

"Not everywhere is like Canterbury," my brother Paul said. He must have read my thoughts!

"Tomorrow they will go into the town and see what food there is for sale," Brother Francis said. "The coast is not far away, and we hope for a plentiful supply of fish, although we will have to walk or ride to Lydd to collect it."

"I've been told that these ditches have a ready supply of eels." A lay monk gestured to the waterway that will round the eastern end of our new church.

"Now that will be useful," Brother Francis responded. "This land looks so barren, but already we believe we can find wood and fish, while eels are here for the catching."

Brother Francis has truly settled into the role of leader and, for now, Brother Fabian does not object. Sometimes, the steward wanders amongst us, the plans for the church in his hands and a frown on his face. I don't know if he realises that the pegs and string mark out an area which is shorter than it should be, or if he is waiting for us to add the aisles. He says little, and I suspect he merely holds the plans to give an impression of being in charge.

His face has a permanent sheen upon it, and his only nourishment is dry bread. I wonder if whatever ails him has led to a lack of appetite or if he is determined to serve penance for losing the gold coins.

Our sickly monk and the lost gold are the only storm clouds hanging over us on this first full day spent at Midley. Everyone else has been engaged in work. The carpenters toiled alongside the unskilled labourers, digging trenches to a depth of three feet and shuttering it with planks. Our first plan was to dig trenches for every wall, but we had not considered that the ground would be so sandy and golden grains would be tumbling back in as we worked. The planks, initially intended for a scaffold, were used to hold back the sand while trenches to the north and east were excavated. Meanwhile, the masons sorted through the wagon of stone from Aldington, keeping the best quality ragstone for the walls above the ground and carrying the most uneven lumps to the edge of the trenches. Some of it came already cut in blocks, whereas most was ragged. By evening, a couple of buckets of quicklime and sand had been mixed and the first foundations were laid along the northern edge.

At the end of the day, when we sat around our fire, bowls of thick pottage on our laps and flatbreads in our hands, Brother Fabian appeared. We fell silent.

"Come and sit with us," Brother Francis offered. "We have a plain stew in the pan. Would you care for some?"

"Nay, my hunger is satisfied with yesterday's bread." He didn't sit but stood observing us before turning towards the sun which spilt its liquid gold and burnt orange across the sky. "I am returning to Canterbury," he said. "I have lost over a third of the gold coins needed to build a church here. I cannot pay for the church Archbishop Sudbury imagined, God rest his soul. I have failed the people of Midley and have failed the archbishop."

Most of us remained silent, while others murmured about him being ill and the loss of the coins an unfortunate accident. There had been no neglect.

"Are you going to tell Prior John?" Brother Francis asked.

"I am."

"Do you want one of us to walk back with you?"

"You are needed here," Brother Fabian replied. "I am going to the place they call Longhouse and will ask if one of the boys will guide me to Ivychurch. From there I will request a guide to Newchurch and so it will continue until I see the towers of our cathedral."

As the sun sets on Midley, it has been decided that Brother Fabian will leave at daybreak. He leaves Brother Francis, Harry Woodman and me in charge of building the stone church.

# Gisella

Four days have passed since the first foundations were laid for our new church. Bernard has been to Ivychurch with the steward and returned home. He reported that the walk was dull with no conversation between himself and Brother Fabian and, once the village was in clear sight, he was told he could return to Midley.

"I would have liked to have seen this cathedral-sized church they are building there," he complained. "But I was no longer needed."

Instead, Bernard was made welcome in the old part of Romney, where they were interested in our church, and he enjoyed a hearty meal before coming home. "And I was able to visit our uncle, who still lives to a ripe old age, but his health fails him."

"Gisella or I can walk there tomorrow," Mother said, "with a basket of our produce."

I smiled my agreement, despite wanting to stay here in Midley.

There is always some excuse for us at Longhouse and those from the neighbouring farms and cottages to wander over to where the new church is being built. The foundations have been created, meaning we can see the size and shape of the nave, chancel and tower.

This morning, I took a bowl of peas as a gift for the lay monks who prepare meals for the church builders. We can spare some of our food when it grows in abundance. Afterwards I lingered to watch the masons at work. Diggory showed me their piles of ragstone and pointed to some already cut into square blocks. "Most need attention though," he told me. "These irregular blocks are fine for the main body of the walls, but all the corners, and the buttresses, need to look just so. I've picked out the stones which Paul and I will work until the lines are sharp and straight."

"When will you do it?" I asked.

"Today," he told me. "Look at the foundations – each wall is ready to be built above the ground, so corner stones are needed."

"How long will this stone last you?"

"Not long," he said. "Ten days, two weeks perhaps."

There has already been a delivery of stone from Aldington. Arriving the day Brother Fabian left, it came by wagons – two of them – and it seems that Midley has been deluged with stone. Heaped in piles, it has been sorted from rubble to square blocks. Nearby, the flint from Lyminge has not yet been touched but, when knapped, its glossy, dark insides will provide details which are both decorative and long-lasting.

"They are preparing to build a couple of low platforms." Diggory saw my attention had turned towards the carpenters who were dragging lengths from their pile of sawn timber.

Glancing back at the foundations, I pictured the scaffold in place and the stone walls, but details of the windows and doorways remained elusive. "It will change so quickly," I mused.

As Diggory and the masons selected the first stones they wanted to work upon, I asked, "Are you missing home?"

This time Paul replied, "Aye, I've left my woman behind. But when I return, I'll have plenty in my purse for a cottage, and we can marry."

I considered this for a moment before replying. "And your work? You were building a city gateway."

"We were rebuilding it," Diggory responded. "This is the first time we have built from scratch."

"It's a fine thing to be doing..." Paul told me, "...to create a new church. I'm not sorry I came, but it's different here. We're used to city life. There's always folk coming and going. They come to the cathedral or to sell produce or to look for work. There's alehouses and market stalls and rooms where people stay. It's never quiet and each day is never the same as the one before."

"I'd like to see it," I replied. "It's always the same here. Only the weather and the seasons change." I paused. "Until you came..."

"I like it here," Diggory announced. "I like these open skies and the fields which stretch forever. Sometimes I'm sure I can smell the sea. I've never been to the coast."

"I have." I grinned, pleased to have experienced something that these city men had not. There was another reason for my feeling merry – whereas Paul had mentioned a woman waiting for him in Canterbury, Diggory had not.

"Gisella! Gisella!"

I turned to see Mother calling but resisted the urge to run back to Longhouse. I doubt the women of Canterbury scamper about the place.

In the evening, our talk was full of the progress on the church and how the first rows of stone were rising above ground level.

"I don't understand why the aisles have not been marked out," Eliot said. "Why have foundations been laid where I would expect to see pillars, not walls?"

"These men are experienced. There must be a reason," my mother replied.

"Although the foundations are laid, the only walls they have started are for the chancel," my father told him. "We'll see the rest take shape soon enough."

"I wonder how far the stone will go," Bernard pondered. "It looks like such a lot, but how many wagonloads will come from Aldington before it's finished?"

"Brother Fabian was to pay for more stone when he stopped at Aldington on his way back to Canterbury," my father reminded us.

"There's a mystery!" Bernard exclaimed. "Why is he returning to Canterbury so soon? He has nothing to report other than their arrival here. If he wanted more stone, then he could have bought it and returned here."

"Didn't he tell you why?" I asked.

"He spoke no more than a dozen words," Bernard retorted. "He was absorbed in his own thoughts. A serious fellow, he is."

We considered this for a moment, but it seemed there was nothing more to be said about the steward. In time we would understand his role in the building of our church, but for now it seemed that he had no part to play other than to negotiate the buying of wood, flint and stone.

The last week had been dry, our land becoming parched, but as we lingered after our supper, we noticed the clouds thickening to the east. As they neared, they took on a curious purple hue. The air chilled and, before those first heavy drops of rain fell, we gathered our plates, beakers and the pan hanging over the fire. Father placed turfs over the glowing

embers, and we fled to the shelter of our home. Looking back from the doorway, we saw the masons running towards the Longhouse barn, no doubt eager to avoid the deluge.

In the house, with the windows shuttered, we relied on light from candles. The air felt thick, and I longed to push back the shutters, allowing both the rain and a fresh breeze in.

We busied ourselves with chores before retreating to our beds for the night.

"I've been thinking..." Father returned to our earlier discussion. "When I passed by earlier, Brother Francis was busy, but he asked if we could meet tomorrow. He has something to tell me, and I can't help thinking there is more to Brother Fabian's absence than we know about."

"That man was not fit to walk back to Canterbury," my mother said, her tone dark. "And whatever ails him, I hope he left none of it here in Midley."

# Brother Francis

Today, our fifth in Midley, is the Sabbath. We started our chores at daybreak with clearing the wooden church of our rolls of bedding and spare clothes. The church was swept, and the door wedged open to allow fresh air to flow in. We left the food, the pans and other cooking implements in place at the back of the church, hoping that Father David would not object. He didn't.

With Brother Fabian gone, us lay monks have slipped into life as lay people, rather than lay monks. At times it is so much simpler to call ourselves Samuel, Leo and Joseph, the 'Brother' cast aside. I find myself preferring plain 'Francis'. Sometimes I think it suits me better.

I have lived at Christ Church Priory since I was twelve years of age and am now twenty-three. As the youngest of seven children, with my father being a ditch clearer and itinerant farm labourer, life felt bleak. We children did what we could to bring food

and fuel to the family home, while father travelled where the work was, usually within our parish of St Marys, sometimes further afield. At times he was gone for days or weeks, but I remember a couple of times when we saw nothing of him for several months and assumed he had passed from this life to a better place.

Like my father, I began to scratch about for work on the land, going from place to place, when news came that workers were needed. On the roadside between the new part of Romney and St Marys there was, and probably still is, a long, low cottage which houses lay monks. I would often linger in the area, watching these fellows methodically tending the land and producing crops. They knew how to get the best from the earth, generously manuring it and taking seed from one farm to use on another. Further afield, monks at Orgarswick had their own chapel, and throughout the Marsh they farmed the land in their orderly way.

I began to envy these men for their knowledge of how to grow precious food, their routines and even their well-laundered and neatly patched habits. When I mentioned this to my father, he saw a way to be released from his seventh burden and suggested we set off to Canterbury, working along the way. The city is rich with priories, but it is Christ Church which owns the land here on Romney Marsh. I presented myself at the gates, in the shadows of the glorious

cathedral, and was accepted into their holy walls. Christ Church has been a sanctuary for me. The days of searching for work are long gone and instead I have tended their plots within the city walls.

Did I realise that in eleven years I would never return to my home? Or that I, who had wandered freely, would be restricted to living under the Rule of St Benedict? I am not complaining. The monks taught me well, and I learned about the soil, the seeds and harvesting from the very best teachers.

Did I think, at twelve years old, that I would never know what it was like to be in the company of women? I thought nothing of it. But I think of it now when my gaze lingers on the sweet Gisella.

Here in Midley, I see a different way of life: people with their own land who tend it themselves and feed their families from it. Back at St Marys, I was too young to aspire to this, but now I wonder if there could have been another path for me.

I digress – here in Midley my thoughts wander more freely than previously.

Before the church service, Edwin came to speak with myself, Diggory and Harry. "We need to talk about the foundations," I said, leading him to the site of the stone church.

"It is all we talk about now," Edwin responded. His words surprised me, but he swiftly corrected himself: "I mean the stone church and all of you working on it."

"You've noticed they're lacking..." I still referred to the foundations.

"We only speak about your progress," he told me. "Midley was a quiet place before you all came."

"Soon people will start talking. They will notice it's not right," Diggory began.

Now we all stood in a line with our backs to the wooden church and our toes against the gash in the land showing where the southern wall of the nave would be – except we had plans showing an aisle extending outwards and columns to support the roof here.

"Notice? You are the experts. We're not checking on your work," Edwin was quick to say.

"We marked the nave out twelve feet shorter than the plans," I began to explain. "And these foundations are for church walls, not aisles. We are not building the church Archbishop Sudbury intended, but a smaller, humbler place."

"And until Brother Fabian returns, or there is word from Canterbury, we will concentrate on the chancel and tower," Harry expanded.

"Why?" Edwin asked.

I began telling him about us leaving Canterbury with a purse full of gold nobles secreted within the folds of the steward's habit, and finishing the tale with: "And the next morning, we learned that twelve coins were lost..."

"He was like a man possessed by the devil himself," Diggory told me. "We, the masons and carpenters, didn't know about the nobles."

"The lay monks didn't know exactly what he had in his purse," I admitted. "It wasn't until they were lost that we learnt how many there were."

I continued the tale, with Diggory and Harry adding in extra details here and there. Finally, Edwin could picture it all: the frantic search for the gold, us staying in Ivychurch for an extra night, the three of us forming a team to lead the men. We finished with the decision to build a lesser church until we knew if the money would be replaced by Prior John.

"Has Brother Fabian gone to look for the gold again, or to tell the prior?" Edwin asked.

"He has gone to Canterbury," I said. "And on the way, he will pay for more stone at Aldington. He has taken two nobles with him."

"Where are the others?" Edwin frowned and paused for a moment. "There are ten left?"

"They are here. We asked Father David to keep them safe for us."

"So, we await news from Canterbury," Edwin said. "How long will that take?"

I shrugged. "I suspect Brother Fabian could take a week or more walking there. His spirits are low, and I believe his pace will be slow. After that... will he return to share Prior John's response, or will

someone else be sent in his place, or a messenger arrive by horse?"

We remained standing by the foundations for the south wall, pondering on these possibilities.

"We at Midley have no desire for a grand edifice," Edwin said. "I once travelled to Ivychurch and was astounded by the size of their church. Their parish may be large, but the population is no more than ours. If you built where you have marked out here, we would be satisfied, but the situation is more complicated."

"Aye, we are honouring Archbishop Sudbury's plans," Harry said. "At least that was the intention."

We fell silent for a moment.

"I wanted to tell you... to explain," I continued. "We can continue with the chancel and tower for a few more days, and then..."

"You'd have to explain to the whole village," Edwin suggested.

"We would."

"Let's wait another week," Edwin advised. "If there is no word from Canterbury, then I'll call a meeting."

That is how we left it. I have tried my best to devote this Sunday to the Lord, and to live by the Rule of St Benedict, but my thoughts are restless and frequently roam. I shall be glad when it is Monday, and all our focus is on the building work.

# Gisella

The men from Canterbury have been with us for almost two weeks now. Our land is parched from the summer sun, crops ripen, and we begin to harvest plump raspberries alongside carrots, turnips and beans. Gossip and speculation have started to flow amongst the people of Midley. Why are the walls being created in such a disorderly manner, they ask. Why have the aisles not been marked out when the tower and nave foundations are in place and the chancel walls stand at two feet high?

It is only us at Longhouse Farm who have been trusted with the truth about the lost coins, and this evening Father decided it was time to speak to Brother Francis again. "Ten days have passed, and there is no news from Canterbury."

"I would not expect a sick man to walk to the city and back that quickly," my mother said.

"Neither would I," Father responded. "But it is important that the people of this parish trust the men who have come to live amongst us, and I fear that trust will be lost if the truth is not told. It may be a week or two before we know if the church will be

built as planned or as a smaller version. In the meantime, if we tell everyone about the lost coins, then the monks, masons and carpenters will have our understanding."

After this, Father strolled over to the wooden church before the monks settled for the night.

"It's difficult for the men in charge," remarked mother as she picked up her mending and settled on a bench in the evening sun. "They left Canterbury as workers and arrived as leaders. They don't have the skills."

"They do have the skills," I objected. "When I hear Diggory speak about everything they do and how he hopes to be a cathedral mason..."

"The skills to lead men," she corrected herself. "Gisella! Do settle to something. You're blocking the light with all your pacing to and fro."

I paused and shielded my eyes, gazing towards the west. He may not have been born a leader, but Diggory was well-liked and respected. I felt certain he would achieve his ambition to work on the cathedral one day. "It seems as if Brother Fabian was unfit to lead the men, even before he became ill."

"We can't know that," Mother cautioned. "We can't know what skills he had. The poor man was so ill, and we can only hope that he has recovered. Don't you have some mending to do? Your dress?"

"Well, I'm certain the men will work better for someone who is as skilled as Diggory... and Harry, of

course. Diggory and Harry will have their respect." I turned back to face my mother and the home. "Aye, I've torn my dress..."

"I would hope Brother Fabian had their respect and will have it if he returns."

Dismissing the sickly steward, my thoughts turned to Brother Francis. "The lay monk, Brother Francis, even he will be accepted as someone who knows this land. He was bold enough to lead them to Midley and is a friendly fellow, even if he has no church-building skills."

"We are lucky to have them. Now, this dress..."

Retreating into the home, I took my dress from a wooden peg and my pouch with needles and thread from the trunk at the end of my bed. Then I settled beside my mother, with the dress on my lap, and allowed my thoughts to roam to the stone church and the men who would build it.

Before long, steady footsteps could be heard. Father walked through the house, joining us as we sat, looking as if all we thought of was our sewing. "Ah! Here you are. I've seen Harry and Brother Francis; Diggory was off somewhere. It's all agreed - I'll speak to the people of Midley in the morning. And those who are not there will hear about it soon enough."

"Where was Diggory?" I asked.

Mother turned to look at me, "Listen to your father, Gisella! He is speaking about the lost nobles and telling everyone the truth."

"I don't know where Diggory is," Father said. "It didn't matter to me, and it doesn't matter to you. One of us needs to check on your uncle in the old part of Romney. Juliana, can you spare Gisella?"

"I can and will be glad to," Mother replied. "She is so restless; the walk will do her good."

After tomorrow it will be easier for the masons and the other men. People will stop probing them about why the church is not being built as expected. They will understand the difficulties faced since the loss of the gold. Diggory can build his walls without people questioning his skills and, with or without the money, I'm sure he'll make a fine job of it. His name, and the others, will become part of the story of Midley to be passed on through the generations. As for me – I'm banished to Romney – for the afternoon at least.

# Brother Francis

Today Edwin Midisle asked that everyone gather outside the church after Mass and began to explain how Brother Fabian had left Canterbury with enough money to fund the building of our church, only to lose over a third of the nobles. At first all their attention was focussed on the lost coins. Questions and opinions flew about, each person talking above their neighbour until the story became twisted and no one knew the truth of it.

Edwin called for order: "Friends and neighbours, how can these good men speak if you will not listen? They did not lose the gold, but they are left to deal with the aftermath. Diggory, can you tell everyone what your plans for the church are."

"We have laid foundations for a church with no aisles," he explained. "But we are reluctant to build the north and south walls until we have news from Canterbury. So that is why we concentrate on the

chancel. If there is no more money, then we cannot afford to build to the plans."

"Can you afford to build a church without the aisles?" someone called.

"Nay," he admitted. "Not to the height and length that Archbishop Sudbury wanted. So, we have also made it twelve feet shorter. But, even then, we will have to look for ways to save money."

"How?" someone else asked.

"By buying stone of a lesser quality," Diggory told him. "We have rubble, flint and stone blocks here. If we were to fetch beach pebbles from this place I hear of..."

"Dengemarsh," someone supplied.

"Dengemarsh!" Diggory grinned his thanks. "Beach pebbles... now they would fill in some gaps and would come at little cost."

"No aisles means less wood, and that's another saving," Harry added. "You can trust us to build you a church you'll be proud of. But it won't be the church you thought you'd be having."

These words were greeted with murmurs of approval. Every day I find myself grateful that Diggory Western and Harry Woodman came to Midley. There's something else I feel grateful about – this opportunity I have been given to lead with them. I could see from the beginning that Brother Fabian felt nervous about the responsibility, but it was not

until sickness overcame him that I was able to show my worth.

Now I stepped forward and spoke. "We must pray that Brother Fabian returns to us in good health, with more coins, or clear guidance from Prior John, but until then we must forge our own path. Some of you have heard that I am from Romney Marsh. I hail from St Marys, over there to the east. I want the best for you all. With Diggory and Harry, and all these men, I will make sure you have a fine church."

The people of Midley spoke amongst themselves for a moment and then someone stepped forward. "Ned Smithy," he said. "Blacksmith. I live just over there." He pointed towards a place they call Hawthorn Corner, to the west of Longhouse Farm. "I'm close enough to keep an eye on things and this is what I'm wondering... I heard that Brother Fabian left for Canterbury some time ago. Did he go through Aldington to buy more stone? There was a delivery on the day he left. Are you expecting more?"

If Ned Smithy had struck me with his hammer, I could not have been more flummoxed. The first delivery of stone arrived within days of us ordering it. Brother Fabian must have passed through Aldington about eight days ago, so where was the stone he had ordered on his return to Canterbury?

"You are right. We are expecting more," I responded. "Brother Fabian did indeed take two nobles as payment for stone. No doubt it will be with

us tomorrow or the day after. And by then, hopefully, word will come from Canterbury, and we will know what is expected from us."

"But until then, you have two less nobles and no stone," Ned Smithy retorted.

"Until then, we have stone paid for and on its way to us," Edwin countered.

I can only pray that Edwin is right.

By evening Edwin had sent a message with his son, Bernard, and asked for a private discussion. We met at his hearth with Diggory and Harry. "I suggest we wait four days," he said. "If we continue at this rate, we'll have a church with no middle. We need to know if Brother Fabian reached Canterbury."

"And if he didn't, where is he?" Harry continued. "Did he get sick again?"

"Someone must find out," my father suggested. "Follow in his footsteps. Is he ill and resting somewhere or did he reach Canterbury? Take my horses – I have two – and you can reach the city within two or three days."

"We can make it in two and a half," I declared. "You're right – we must send two men, or we could be at risk of losing another! Edwin, you're a good friend to us. Thank you!"

"I think you should go, Francis," Diggory suggested.

"Me?" I pondered on this. "I suppose I must do what is best for Midley, and you are both needed here. Who shall I take with me?"

"Take my son, Bernard," Edwin offered. "He would enjoy the adventure. What do you think, Bernard?"

"What do I think?" Bernard replied, a grin on his face. "If you can spare me, I'll go to Canterbury."

"We may have news of Brother Fabian before that," I said. "But most likely we'll be riding to Canterbury."

"Where will he stay?" Edwin asked. "Once you are in Canterbury, I mean."

"Go to my brother, Mark," Diggory said. "He lives near West Gate. Just ask for Mark Western and say I sent you."

Darkness has enveloped the land, and I feel certain I will return to Canterbury soon as Brother Francis. Already I feel stifled by those walls, the bells and the routines. What about Bernard, Eliot and Gisella? Where are their places in this world? Three hundred years ago their ancestors were among the first to settle here, but some Midley folk will move away and, in turn, new blood will come. Will any of them choose to leave?

# Brother Francis

For the first time in a decade, I find myself without the company of monks. Instead, I am with Bernard, a young man with a winning smile and enthusiasm for this journey. We talk about my early life on the Marsh and how I journeyed to Canterbury escorted by my father. My introduction to the monks at Christ Church was through the priest's cousin, a quire monk who, at the time, was a daunting character. But, amongst those silent, tonsured figures, I noticed the lay monks working on the land outside the city walls and bustling about within the cathedral precincts. I saw a life in which, if I worked for the community, I would always be fed and housed.

In turn, Bernard tells me about his life in Midley and the places he has been. The family are unusually well-travelled, having journeyed by boat along a creek, known as the Wainway, to Rye in the west, and as far east as a fishing village named Dymchurch. Mostly their lives revolve around the weather and

the changing seasons. This is the life I would have led if I had stayed in St Marys, rarely going further than the next parish.

Following in the footsteps of Brother Fabian, we rode to Ivychurch and then Newchurch on the first day. Here we paused to eat bread and cheese supplied by Juliana.

"Aye, we saw him," the people of Newchurch said. "It was two weeks ago, perhaps a little less. Perhaps a little more."

"How was he?" I asked.

"My wife gave him some ale," the reeve said. "He slept in our barn overnight and was gone in the morning. We offered to feed him, but he declined."

"Your steward was like a shadow passing through," the priest offered in an oddly poetic way. "He prayed at length in the church and asked for nothing but weak ale to quench his thirst."

We rode on to Bilsington and learned that Brother Fabian had called in to St Augustine's Priory. "He prayed in our chapel and drank water from our well," the prior told us. "I would have liked him to stay in our infirmary, to rest for a few days, but he was intent on returning to Canterbury."

At the end of our first day, we arrived at Aldington and headed for the quarry.

"He's not been here," the foreman insisted. "I know the fellow you mean, and he has not been here. You've had the wagons of stone paid for when you all

98

passed though. When was that? Almost a cycle of the moon ago? There have been no more monks here since then."

"But he was at Bilsington." My words sounded foolish.

"Bilsington is Bilsington," the foreman retorted. "He's not been here."

"That's two more nobles gone," Bernard muttered darkly.

Before I left Midley, Diggory and Harry had insisted that I take two nobles with me. "We need more good stone for the doorways and window dressings," Diggory told me. "The alternative would be to use wood, but..." He waved his hand towards the clump of trees growing near Longhouse Farm. "There is little wood here and whether it is timber or stone, it has to come from off the Marsh."

Reluctantly, I parted with the two nobles, and it was arranged that two wagons of stone would leave for Midley at first light.

"Let's speak to the men who will take it and ask them to pass on a message," Bernard suggested.

The message was simple: "Brother Fabian has not reached Aldington. We are continuing to Canterbury."

With my spirits low, I heaved myself onto the horse once more and turned his nose towards the church and the Archbishop's Palace where I would ask for a

bed and nourishment. Bernard was subdued, but this great adventure was not over for him, and I sensed he was attempting to contain his enthusiasm for the next step.

Aldington's church and palace buildings were built alongside each other, the palace being part of the churchyard boundary. Here we saw a wealth of barns, stables and cottages as well as a manor house.

I found it tiring to be forced to explain the reason for us travelling through but didn't have the energy to come up with some untruth that probably wouldn't stand up to their friendly questioning. At least Bernard and I were fed well and offered comfortable pallets for the night.

Now, as the sun sets in the direction of Romney Marsh, I am drawn to their church. For the first time in weeks, I feel that I could take some comfort from prayer. Perhaps He can guide me over the coming days. In two days, we will be in Canterbury and the responsibility of recounting the tale of the lost nobles weighs heavy upon me.

Where is Brother Fabian? If he chose to flee, then I cannot blame him. If I didn't have the responsibility of young Bernard, then maybe I would do the same. I am being foolish. In the morning, my thoughts will be clearer and spirits lifted.

# *Brother Francis*

## Canterbury

Bernard and I have ridden since dawn on the stocky ponies belonging to his father. In the heat of the midday sun, we rested in the shade then mounted the reluctant beasts once more. It is too much for these ponies which are used to working the land at Midley, or taking the tracks to Lydd or Romney, but we have travelled to Canterbury in two-and-a-half days and are grateful for that.

We approached the city by Stone Street, then, having passed Lower and Upper Hardres, dismounted to lead the ponies up the hill. At the top, I couldn't help being filled with a sense of awe as I looked down on the city, dominated by the cathedral.

"Is this it?" Bernard asked. "Canterbury?"

"This is it," I replied.

He fired questions at me – where was this and that... what was this... what was that... I answered the best I could, but it was hard to tell one place from the next at this distance. We rode on, and I learnt, with surprise, that Bernard had seen town walls and gates before, from his two trips to Rye. Of course, everything about Canterbury was larger and finer than Rye, but he was eager to compare the two.

Outside the city, I left the ponies with a farmer I knew – a friendly chap whose land runs alongside priory fields. Then Bernard and I walked to the city walls, entering through Worth Gate, with the Norman castle dominating the ground to our left.

My feelings were mixed as we walked along the city street, with houses, taverns and workplaces jostling against each other. At first came pride in being able to call this place my home, and excitement to be back where there are always people to be seen, buildings being created or reworked, and news from afar to be shared. Then my nose began to twitch as an old hag pushed a barrow of decaying cabbages past me, a scraggy dog at her heels, and having side-stepped her, the toes of my shoes touched upon a stream of... of... But before I could consider this and warn Bernard to be careful, a women stepped out of her doorway and flung a bucket of dirty water into the open drain.

The clear skies and fresh breezes at Midley beckoned me, and Canterbury no longer held any appeal.

The questions ceased to flow from Bernard. He walked close to me, observing as much as he could. I began to doubt the wisdom of bringing this lad to the city. As we reached the main thoroughfare, stretching to our left and right, the cathedral gate could be spied at the end of the narrow lane running straight ahead.

"Is that it? Is that the cathedral?" he asked.

"It is. But I need to make an appointment to see the prior. You must go to Diggory Western's family."

"I could have a quick look."

I couldn't refuse him that, so we went and stood for a moment at the Christ Church gateway, and he was silent once more. At first, I thought Bernard should be guided through the intricate tracery, carved figures, elaborate pinnacles and ancient Norman features. But where to begin? So much to see, and an introduction to the Westerns beckoned. Instead, I let him stand and gaze without intrusion from me.

"I'll be able to see it again, won't I?" he asked. Then, before I could answer, "Where do you live? Where are the monks?"

"You will." I smiled, and continued, "On the north side there are kitchens, dining rooms, dormitories

and offices. An infirmary and rooms where they make books. It's like another town, but different."

"How?"

"It's orderly and silent – almost silent. We live by routines and the pattern of the day rarely falters."

"Do you go in there a lot?" he asked, nodding towards the cathedral.

"I do, but not as often as the quire monks. I usually work on the vegetable plots." I paused, before reminding him, "We must find the Westerns now, then I'll make an appointment to see Prior John."

Bernard didn't ask why. He knew about the nobles.

As we returned to the main street, my young companion turned his attention to West Gate, knowing that Diggory and Paul Western were part of the team who had rebuilt this robust city gateway. We went directly to the gate, assuming that Mark Western would still be at work and wanting to catch him before he left for his home or the alehouse.

A lad fetched Mark, who was immediately recognisable with the same golden curls and pleasant face as his younger brothers.

"Has something happened to them?" he asked. "Are you one of them who went to Romney Marsh?"

"They are fine," I replied. "But aye, I have come from Midley. I'm Brother Francis and this is Bernard Midisle. Your brothers are both living with Bernard's family and the message from them is that all is well."

"Thank the saints for that," Mark responded. "We worried about them going off like that."

Had I been Brother Fabian then I may have told him that it was God's will, but instead I continued with practical matters: "I must see the prior, and tomorrow we'll return to Midley. Your brothers suggested that Bernard could stay with you and your family?"

"Of course!" Mark replied immediately. "Our home is humble, but you are welcome."

We agreed that Mark would bring Bernard back to West Gate in the morning and he would wait as long as necessary until I had been granted an interview with Prior John.

"If there are any delays I'll send a message for you," I concluded.

With that I left, once more walking along the wide St Peter Street, against the flow of market traders and labourers who were leaving the city centre at the end of their day's work.

A sense of peace wrapped around me as I stepped through the gateway at the eastern end of the cathedral and into the priory grounds. Work on the nave had finished for the day. Muted sounds came from the movement of monks as they went about their duties.

My body returned to its previous way of being – head slightly bowed, shoulders rounded – and when

I passed another person, I merely nodded. Here in Christ Church Priory, we did not call to one another across the cloisters or chatter for no good reason. Subduing my natural urges to be free with my speech and gestures, I strolled along the paths to our chapel and knelt before the altar, hoping to reconnect with my life as a monk.

After a while I rose and considered the time. I had heard the bell ring for the mid-afternoon prayer called None while I stood at the cathedral gateway with Bernard. After that, some of the monks would have spent time in the chapter house, listening to a reading from the Rule of St Benedict before discussing any important business. By now they would be leaving, and I could see if Prior John or another senior monk was available.

On the green between the chapel and the cathedral, all was peaceful. I hastened towards the chapter house, following the corridors under the treasury, and the prior's private chapel, through the locutorium, where we were allowed to talk without restriction, and towards the great cloister. Monks spilt out, walking with purpose in all directions. *How am I to find the prior? And if I do, how to approach him?* I faltered, and at that moment a young monk went to pass by me but stopped and asked, "Brother Francis, is that you? Let us bless the Lord."

Placing my hands together as if to pray, I nodded and responded with, "Thanks be to God. Brother

Michael, I am returned from Midley and need an audience with Prior John."

"Alone?" Brother Michael whispered.

"Alone other than being with a lad from Romney Marsh who accompanied me and is now with the Westerns."

"I'll speak with the prior after Vespers," Brother Michael told me. "Let's meet after supper."

"Thank you."

We separated and I slipped into the routines of the monastic life, first attending vespers in the cathedral and then supper. One lay monk looks very like the next and there is nothing about me to make me stand out, other than my pale red hair, but I knew some of my companions would recognise me and be both surprised and confused by my return to Christ Church. I kept my eyes cast down and hoped to avoid any more whispered questions – Prior John must be told the reason for my being here before anyone else.

I ate supper, one of a line of monks sitting at the far end of the refectory. A well-schooled quire monk read from the Scriptures. My thoughts drifted to our mealtimes at Midley: plates balanced on our laps while we sat on low benches in a companionable circle, chattering about our day. I felt the sun on my skin and the grass tickling my toes; I smelt the woodsmoke drifting from the fire and the dry grass in nearby meadows. A pang of regret at leaving my temporary home hit me hard, leaving a physical

effect – a heaviness in my limbs and a dullness of mind. Taking a long draft of ale, I forced myself to return to the present.

Afterwards, I lingered outside the refectory, my gaze fixed on the ground. I didn't know Brother Michael stood beside me until he spoke: "Prior John will see you now. Wait outside his chambers."

I murmured my thanks and plodded along the ancient stone walkways and corridors to the prior's chambers. Then I waited outside, leaning gently against the cool wall. The prior soon approached, his pace steady. As he neared me, he placed his hands together and bowed until his fingertips touched his forehead. I repeated the gesture.

"Brother Francis, please come into my chamber." He led the way up a stone staircase, opened an ancient oak door and we stepped into a dimly-lit room. Prior John seated himself in a carver chair. I knelt for his blessing which he gave before stating, "You come with news."

"Brother Fabian is missing," I began as I stood. "At least I believe him to be. He has not returned here?"

"He has not. Missing from where?"

"Romney Marsh, I think, or at least the hills bordering it. When we left Canterbury, we travelled to Lyminge, then Aldington and Bilsington, through Newchurch and to Ivychurch. On that last afternoon, Brother Fabian was struck down with fever. I know the Marsh and led the men to Ivychurch. They

welcomed us, and our brother took to his bed. None of us knew that he carried a purse of gold nobles, but the next day he was distraught – the purse had broken and many of the nobles were lost. Half our men searched the countryside but with no joy. The others remained in Ivychurch, working in exchange for our food and bed. Eventually we continued to Midley. Brother Fabian's fever had passed but he was laid low with lethargy. After a day in Midley, he left bound for Canterbury."

"How did you know he had gone missing?"

"He took two nobles with him, and we were expecting a delivery of more stone. It didn't arrive. So, I followed in his footsteps. He was seen at Newchurch and Bilsington, but never arrived at Aldington."

"May God look kindly upon his troubled soul," Prior John murmured. "How many coins have been lost?"

"Twelve, then two more that were meant for the new stone. Fourteen. We need to know how to proceed. For now, Midley church is being built without aisles. There is no money for the stone." I didn't mention that it was also twelve feet shorter. "We don't know if the nobles will be found or replaced." I paused. "Please forgive my... my blunt speech. We have masons, carpenters and labourers but can't build with the little stone and wood we have."

"I understand. You speak of 'we'. Who is taking charge now Brother Fabian is gone?"

"Diggory Western and Harry Woodman – both skilled and respected – and… and myself, due to my knowledge of the Marsh."

"Does it work well, this trio of men?"

"It does," I told him. "Very well."

"Our steward is missing, along with fourteen gold coins."

"Not together!" I hastened to add. "No one thinks that. He was so ill… He is missing with two gold coins; the others are lost."

"Nevertheless, I need to think. Come back tomorrow."

Now I am in my dormitory, lying on my mattress. The air stifles me and sleep evades me. It is not yet fully dark, and I gaze at the rafters, following their lines until they fade away at the end of the room. I believe that my companions are asleep, although it has taken some time for them to settle – most were curious to learn why I had returned but thwarted by my reluctance to share the story of the lost coins. Who knows where Brother Fabian is, but I know that I mustn't speak of his illness, the desperate search for the gold and the malady of his mind that followed. I picture myself in a different place and, instead of breathing in the scent of ancient stone, I smell the earth and seasoned planks of the wooden church at

Midley. I picture fields of wheat and barley ready to harvest and buzzards hovering above, the reed-lined dyke curving around the 'nose' of the original Middle Isle, and the turquoise dragonflies darting about.

# Brother Francis

"There is to be no more gold for Midley."

Once more Prior John sat behind his desk, and I stood before him. The only difference was that this time the early morning light came through the heavily mullioned windows facing to the east.

I waited.

"You speak of this team of skilled men who now lead the project. Let them find a way of building a church with what the land provides. Or find the lost gold. I have looked at maps of Romney Marsh and there is no distance between Newchurch and Ivychurch. If the nobles fell from a broken purse as you said, then they are there to be found. As for Brother Fabian, do not concern yourself with him. I will send a party of monks to Bilsington Priory and seek their help."

"Very well. A church to match Archbishop Sudbury's plans?" I queried, keeping my voice steady while my thoughts raced.

"A stone church constructed as well as it can be with sixteen nobles," Prior John stated.

"Do you have any directions for the men back at Midley?"

"Look at the current church – can any of the materials be reused? And I hear Rye has supplies of brick in a yard by the shore. It is much cheaper than stone. Above all, if you follow His guidance, then all will be well. Is there anything else, Brother Francis?"

My mouth dried. Pictures of my return to Midley with no gold and little guidance flooded my mind. Prior John had clearly finished, yet so little had been discussed.

"Is there anything else?" the prior repeated.

Before I could stop myself, I replied, "I wish to return to Romney Marsh as Francis. Or even plain Frank. To no longer be Brother Francis. And, when the church at Midley is built, to stay there or some other place nearby and farm the land."

"How long have you been considering this?"

"A year or more, but I knew little of life beyond this city. Now I do and it is a life I want to be a part of."

"Would you like to be counselled?" he asked.

"Nay, my decision has been made," I replied before I could stop myself.

"You no longer wish to be bound by the holy Rule of St Benedict, and to be released from your vows?"

"I wish to be released."

"Then may God be with you wherever you are in this land, and may the lessons learned from Saint Benedict stay with you."

"Thank you, Prior. May God be with you." Kneeling, I bowed my head for his final blessing upon me.

I left, walking for the last time down the stone pathways and corridors of Christ Church Priory towards the store where a monk oversaw trunks containing the shifts, tunics and capes worn by lay people. Then as a man, not a monk, I stepped into the bright sunlight of the cathedral grounds and walked out of the Christ Church gateway. I did not look back. Not once. My friend, Bernard Midisle, was waiting for me at West Gate and I was determined not to keep him waiting.

# Gisella

## Midley

Now our lives fit into two parts – before they came, and after. Today there was yet another twist to my story of these men from Canterbury and the church they are building. Brother Francis is now just Francis or Frank! He is still in the heart of it all and will work with the lay monks, but when the church is complete and the men leave, he will make his own way in the world. I know that Bro… Frank's family came from St Marys, a place not so far away, but don't know if he will return there. He told us that he went to Canterbury because there was not enough work to provide for him and his family, and I assume nothing has changed. They are not farmers like us, but labourers who work the land when and where they are needed.

Perhaps Frank will be an itinerant worker, travelling from one place to another. He would be free, no longer bound to the Church and the order of St Benedict. But I have a feeling… I am quite sure that

Frank wants to settle somewhere and make it his home. There may be an opportunity for him here at Midley, but our parish is small, and I cannot see that any of the farmers here could keep a worker who is not a family member. Like us at Longhouse Farm, they have their own sons.

Frank stands taller now and his smile is broader. He shares a firm friendship with Bernard, having spent four days with him. Bernard also looks more confident, as one minute he speaks of the glorious cathedral and the grand buildings in the city, but the next of the stinking gullies, a filthy river and people crammed into cottages which are, in turn, crammed together, one beside the other. He exaggerates – I am certain of it. My brother is, like me, unused to city life.

"How do we travel to Rye?" Frank asked my father, when Prior John's response to the loss of the nobles had been shared. "We cannot afford to build this church from stone, not even rubble, and I have been told there are bricks in Rye."

"There are," Father responded. "I have seen them for myself. They will be mis-matched as they arrive as ballast on ships. They may have been re-used several times and will have suffered for being knocked about but, you're right, there are bricks in Rye."

"I've been to Lydd in your absence," Diggory told Frank. "People here also use beach pebbles, along with rubble, to build walls."

"Bricks are half the price of stone, and pebbles come at little cost, but we would have to ask permission from the bailiff of Lydd."

"I need stronger beams than those currently in the wooden church," Harry said. "Although I'll do my best to reuse wood from there as the new church progresses, for now we can't take apart the place you sleep in. The main beams must be new wood – or new to us – and strong; that's what's needed. I'll need to go back to Bilsington for it."

"What about the holly wood on the shingle beyond Lydd?" Father asked. "Even if it is no cheaper, it will not have to be transported as far and may be of use for decorative features."

"It is cheaper and a fine-grained, hard wood – a pleasure to work with. I've already spoken to the chap who manages it," Harry replied.

"You asked how to travel to Rye," Father returned to Frank's query. "You've not seen much of this parish yet, but if you follow the tracks to the south-west, to the Agney Marshes, there's a channel known as Wainway and before long it's wide and deep enough to take a fishing boat. We'll find some fellow down there who will take us to Rye at high tide. Rye's on a hill, you see, and the place is almost surrounded by mud at low tide. At high tide, it's almost an island.

There's a strand and warehouses and plenty of trading going on."

"You said 'we' and 'us'." Frank grinned.

"I'll go with you," Father said. "And you, Diggory. No good a farmer and a ... a ... Frank choosing bricks. You need to be happy with them."

"And when we've bought the brick? Will it come by boat?" Diggory asked.

"Aye, it will have to," Father responded. "Those heavy horses you brought here with you, they can wait near the creek with your wagons. It will take every man you have and any Midley men who can be spared when it comes to moving the bricks. There's no harbour down there and the ground will be soft, so there will be some distance to cover from the boat to the wagons."

"Or we could lay planks down?" Harry suggested.

And so the conversation passed between the men. One moment they were speaking of our new church, the next about the trip to Canterbury, with Bernard adding a little here and there. My brother felt his new experiences entitled him to be treated as an equal amongst the men, and I couldn't help but agree. The whereabouts of Brother Fabian was discussed at length.

"Should some of us go and search for him?" Harry wondered. "I feel a responsibility. We shouldn't have let him leave when he was so ill."

"None of us could tell him what to do," Diggory pointed out. "But I agree with you."

"I believe Prior John will send a party of monks to search the area," Frank said. "He spoke of them going to Bilsington and engaging the help of the monks there."

"Were they to go immediately?" Father asked.

"It was not for me to suggest it," Frank admitted. "My audience with him was brief."

Mother and I listened in, fascinated by their discussion and plans. By the end of the evening, it had all been agreed. Tomorrow Father, Frank and Diggory will travel to Rye. They will take Eliot who deserves his own adventures.

# Diggory

The walls of our chancel now reach my chest. This has been the easy part – building the walls with rubble and making neat corners with cut stone. As I leave Midley for Rye, Paul is about to start working the ragstone to create the windowsill, and now our progress will be slower as each block is shaped, and the mullions rise, tall and slim. We have decided that the chancel window, with its three apertures, will be the only one to fulfil Archbishop Sudbury's vision. Glass is expensive and a luxury we can barely afford. The nave windows will be humble versions of those planned and left unglazed.

I am relieved that we now know the fourteen nobles are lost: the twelve which fell from Brother Fabian's purse between Newchurch and Ivychurch, and the two he had with him when he set off for Canterbury. When I say 'relieved', I do not mean it to sound as if I am *pleased* they are gone. I mean that we now know that the church must be built as a humble place with a nave and chancel. To add a tower is ambitious. After much discussion, we – Frank, Harry and myself – have decided to reduce the

size of the tower once more. Thankfully, we had concentrated on building the chancel and only the tower foundations were in place. It is to be a mere eight feet square – enough to hold a bell and no more.

A bell! It is too much. I can only hope that Canterbury will fund this.

Today, little work will progress here at Midley. Frank and I are off to Rye, while Harry, two masons and all four labourers have left for Aldington and Bilsington with our heavy horses and the wagons. Two precious nobles go with them, and the men will return with both ragstone and timber – they will carry less on each wagon this time, making it easier to negotiate the hillside track and bridge across the Rhee. Although I am heading off in search of brick, we know we must buy more stone and wood. This is the last ragstone we will buy.

When Paul begins to chip away at the stone, ensuring it is smooth and straight and the corners are crisp, the other masons will be lifting some of the tower foundations, chipping off the mortar and digging fresh trenches. I know they will find it frustrating, but we must reduce the size of the tower. Harry has suggested that rather than its being tall and square, it could be topped with a spire covered in wooden shingles. "We can make shingles from wood that may otherwise be burned on the fire," he said yesterday.

The women of Midley and the lay monks here would be glad of that firewood!

We usually rise not long after dawn but are in no rush and amble across to the church at our own pace. These summer days are long, and we put in many hours of work. Today we must make haste to catch the tide when it rises in the Wainway creek. Rye beckons us and I am curious to see the town with its rich history and stores of bricks.

# Gisella

My brother Eliot asked if he could join the trek to the hills and back rather than come to Rye with us. So, I went to Rye with the men, carrying a basket with packages of bread, cheese and handfuls of fresh lettuce leaves. The men took their own flasks of weak ale. It seemed as if the whole of Midley came to life early this morning as so many of us set off in opposite directions.

My father led the way. Before long, we were scrambling up a bank and walking along a raised pathway in the direction of Agney Marsh and the Wainway. The bank, one of several, tells the story of our part of Romney Marsh and is an ancient seawall. Further towards the coast there lies another and another, each one showing how the tidal marshland has been reclaimed and farmed. As reeve of our parish, my father keeps a close eye on these earth walls for any signs of a fracture. The sea cannot be trusted to stay in its place, so occasionally a wall is breeched and land lost.

I stray. On this summer's day, those winter storms are a long way off. By the time we are forced to stay in our homes by lengthy nights and harsh weather, the men from Canterbury will have retreated to their city and Midley will, once more, be a lonely place.

We walked, with Father pointing out landmarks along the way, but mostly left to our own thoughts. Men do not chatter when there is nothing important to say. We reached the Wainway, at first no more than a narrow ditch, choked with reeds and the water lying stagnant. It widened, and I spotted the sea forging along the channel, bringing life to the sluggish waters and pressing upon the upright reed stems. On we went, and I think we all found the swirling, rising tide hypnotic to watch. In time, the Wainway seemed both wide and deep enough to take a small vessel, and before long we came across a fisherman with his boat securely fastened to a hawthorn tree.

"Greetings, Joe." Father raised his hand. "Thank you for meeting us. You know my daughter, Gisella. These are the men from Canterbury – Diggory and Frank."

"You're the ones building a church then." Joe eyed them curiously. "Which one of you was the monk?"

We don't talk about it back in Midley, at least not openly.

"It was me," Frank said. "But I'm a Marsh man. From St Marys."

"Oh! From St Marys, are you? I'm a Lydd man."

Joe had been neatly distracted, and my father said, "Is the tide high enough?"

The fisherman studied the water in a manner which irritated me. He knew the Wainway and the tides. This creek ran through his blood, as they say.

"It will do," he responded. "But when we're there, you won't have long to see them bricks you spoke about."

"Bricks are bricks," Diggory told him. "As long as there's a fellow there to take our money and arrange delivery, then it won't take long to do the deal."

I smiled to myself, liking his confident manner.

"Let's get on with it." Father gestured to a platform at the water's edge, then asked Joe, "Can you hold the boat steady while we get on?" He looked at me. "Gisella, you can sit this end with Diggory."

I followed his thinking – my father had placed me where he would be sitting between me and Joe Rother. Although happy to include me in this adventure, he too felt a dislike for the man who we were relying on to take us to Rye. After some shuffling about in the boat, and some mutterings from Joe about whether the water was high enough, and that four passengers was a lot for his small vessel, we set off with Frank taking the second oar.

Sitting within a hair's breadth of Diggory, with the early morning sun on our backs, and the water sparkling as it fell from the oars, I felt as if I were heading towards a great adventure.

The Wainway widened, then joined the even broader Rother estuary, an area both dangerous and fascinating. Great bars of sand were fast becoming swallowed up by the sea, yet would lie there awaiting ships who may be unaware of how to negotiate a safe passage through. Joe with his flat-bottomed boat, felt no fear. By now the sail had been raised, hastening our progress despite us moving against the wind. Joe showed his skill by angling the sail this way and that, taking us from one side of the channel to the other, but all the time in the direction of Rye. To the west, towards Winchelsea, merchant ships lay at anchor in the deeper harbour; I wondered where they came from and what they carried.

"Do you know Rye?" Diggory asked, distracting me from thoughts of faraway lands.

The town sat on a hill overlooking the estuary where three rivers joined and flowed to the coast. Almost an island, I knew it to be a centre for trading, but also many battles with the French. The men of Rye and nearby Winchelsea were known to be a ruthless lot with hatred simmering within them; they did not hesitate to retaliate when the French raided the town.

"We went there once when I was much younger," I told him. "Then again last year. It was horrible that second time, after the raids. So much damage..."

"Damage?"

"Fire. Almost burned to the ground," I told him. "Although three years had passed, the walls were still scarred from the flames and many properties had not been cleared or rebuilt. They had been to France and brought the church bells back though."

"They?"

"The men of Rye and Winchelsea. The bells were taken, you see..."

"I'm beginning to!" He grinned, but then his expression became serious. "What made you go to such a place? Were you safe?"

"I think so... We didn't stay overnight. It was like today – Father wanted to buy something and organised for it to be delivered."

"I wonder why they took the church bells," Diggory mused.

"I don't know... Perhaps just because they could?"

We sat in silence for a moment. I think we were both thinking about the French travelling along this same stretch of water, intent on causing havoc. Perhaps it was my imagination, but I sensed that something shifted in my growing friendship with Diggory. I sensed that my stories of Rye had caused him to feel protective towards me. Every so often our arms and legs pressed against each other with the

movement of the boat, and I found myself liking the closeness. At first, we apologised to each other, but there was nothing to be done about it, so in time we shrugged and smiled.

With the tide surging up the estuary, the sailing boat was pushed on her way towards the town's beach. My attention turned to the details in the stonework of Rye's town walls wrapping themselves around the hill, the Ypres Tower rising above them, a fortified gateway and, topping them all, the church.

"I can't see where we'll moor," Diggory said.

"That way." I pointed to the left. As I did so, the boat turned to follow a channel between two sandbanks.

"You'll take care, won't you?" he replied, and I realised Diggory was still thinking of the possible dangers in Rye. "Make sure you're with your father or me at all times."

"Or Frank," I suggested, partly to see the response.

"I'm not sure he knows enough of the world... of what men can be like," Diggory replied. "Although you couldn't find a better fellow."

"Or Joe?" I looked towards the fisherman as he concentrated on lowering the sail and took both oars.

"I can't say I take to him." Diggory's eyes narrowed. "He thinks too much of himself and for no good reason."

"I'll stay with my father... or you."

"Thank you." I was rewarded with a smile.

The boat lurched and his body was thrown against mine. I didn't complain!

As we neared the fishermen's beaches, my gaze took in a hotchpotch of wooden warehouses, net sheds and yards. Gulls swooped and screamed while fishing smacks unloaded their catch, and carts took the fish the short distance to the market. Beyond this, I glimpsed the ancient sea cliffs which told the story of ancient times when the sea came up to them.

Negotiating other vessels, Joe guided his boat towards the beach until the hull ground into the sand. "Can I leave her here?" he called to a well-weathered chap who looked as if he belonged to the town's fishing community. "It's not for long."

"Aye, if you speak to the Master over yonder. It will cost you a grout, or a penny if he's feeling generous. I'll help you pull her in a bit."

"Thank you." Joe turned back to us. "Out you get. We'll pull her up together. I'm off to catch up with my cousin, but don't be long. I want to leave shortly after the tide turns." As he gave his orders, we clambered out and into the shallows.

"We won't be long," Father confirmed. I could feel he was irritated by this. We live near enough to the sea and the tidal creeks to understand the tides. Besides, Joe had already discussed this while we were sailing towards Rye.

With Joe sauntering away, we moved away from the river and followed a track, with the undercliff towering above us. Men moved to and from warehouses and yards, pushing carts or carrying sacks and crates. They called to each other – barking orders and exchanging greetings. Amongst them, elderly men squatted on stools fixing nets or watching life go by and offering the benefit of their wisdom. This was a man's place, and I stayed next to Father, with Diggory and Frank close behind us.

Every so often I spotted a woman, weather-beaten with ragged clothes, usually carrying a basket of fish. Occasionally a girl darted through the place, perhaps carrying a message or buying fish for her mother. The women, I assumed, would be in the town – busy with the children, keeping the house in order and ensuring a hearty meal simmered in the pot.

They say that every old place in Rye was burned down by the French, so new homes have risen from the cellars upwards. I'd have loved to have seen what a new town looks like, everything fresh within the ancient town walls. But we were there to view bricks, and Father led us to a yard where several men were browsing the brick and stone. The owner looked on as he sat on a bench, a beaker of ale in his hand, an open shelter shading him from the sun.

Diggory immediately went to the stone, and I followed. "Scorched!" he said.

"From the fire," I reminded him.

"Of course. But it's good stuff. At least some of it is." Diggory ran his fingertips over a carved block. "Brick will be cheaper." He turned away and joined the others.

I lingered, looking for the cut stone amongst the rubble, wondering where it had stood before the French destroyed so much of the town.

My attention turned to a staircase, part wood, part cut into the cliff, rising steeply behind us. *This must lead to the town. I wonder what it's like up there.* Taking a few steps towards the stairs, I looked up, noting how they turned this way and that, so no section was the same as the next.

Glancing back, I saw Father, Diggory and Frank examining the brick, and the man getting up from his bench to amble towards them. *If I went to that second platform, then perhaps I could see something of the new town and it's only a few steps away. They'll still know where I am.* I darted up the first set of steps. Now as high as the roof of the wooden shelter in the yard, I could see waves breaking on the beach and boats bobbing up and down with the swell.

The staircase remained clear from top to bottom, so I ran up the next stairs. Now I could see the harbour and merchant ships at anchor, and the shapes of sandbars under the tidal waters. In the distance, a ribbon of sea sparkled. Below, in the yard, Diggory spoke to the man and pointed to various

bricks. All was quiet on the stairs. *One more ... if I go to the next platform, then maybe...*

I scampered up to the third platform. The view of the sea became clearer, and I spotted a couple of larger ships in the bay. To my right, neighbouring Winchelsea perched on its hilltop. I frowned, turning my attention back to the coast, wondering if there was any sign of Old Winchelsea, destroyed by storms in the last century. The light on the sea made it difficult to know if the distant sandbank held traces of the old town. Or was it the masts of a ship further out to sea? I narrowed my eyes.

It took a moment for me to become aware of a scuffle above, and by the time I looked up, a young lad had already reached the fourth platform and was racing down to the third. He jumped, falling into me, pushing me against the cliff face and on he went... Hot on his heels, a larger lad leapt down the steps, taking several at a time. "I'll get you, Jem Fisher!" he hollered, passing me as I braced myself and pressed back against the cliff. The smaller one, Jem, disappeared as he leapt from the second platform into the yard. Before I could put a hand up to rub my bruised shoulder, a third came crashing down.

This lad, tall and lean, seemed to be the first to notice me, or at least the first to pause rather than continue the pursuit. "Hurt, are you?" he asked, but where his words should have been kindly, they were uttered with a hint of menace.

"Just a bruise," I lied, my shoulder throbbing.

"I'll take you up to me Ma." He jerked his head upwards, a glint in his eyes.

"I've got to go."

"Not before I've had a kiss," he said, stepping forward, placing a hand on my waist.

Already flattened against the cliff, my heart pounding and the bruised shoulder forgotten, I snapped, "Let me go!" I pushed forward, aiming for the small gap between him and the steps heading back down.

His hand brushed against my back as I jumped the first few steps, stumbled down the next few, put my hand to the cliff face to regain my balance and stifled a scream. Someone else was standing on the steps before me.

"Slow down."

"Sorry."

Diggory shielded me as 'Lean Lad' clattered down the stairs, continuing his pursuit of Jem. Perhaps Diggory gave a push, perhaps it was just awkward to negotiate the narrow stairs. As he passed us, this third lad lost his footing and tumbled down to the second platform. We looked down in horror, and now I realised that my father, Frank, Harry and the brick seller were all staring up.

"I'm sorry," I said again, conscious of Diggory's closeness and the pain in my shoulder.

Having bellowed his fury, the lad pulled himself upright, shot us a look of anger and stepped onto a low edge in the cliff before jumping down and landing behind the brick seller's shelter. From there he disappeared into the shadows as he rounded the bottom of the cliff.

"Did he hurt you?"

"Not him. It was the first one who pushed into me." I put my hand to my shoulder.

"Come on. Let's get you down, and if you need something... some woman to look at it, perhaps..."

"Nay, we have hyssop balm at home."

Once back in the yard, I assured Father that, although bruised, I was fine. He's not a man to fuss, but I'm sure he was grateful to Diggory.

"That's no place for you," the brick seller muttered a few times. "It's for Rye folk. Those who know the town."

"Sorry," I repeated. "Sorry." If we had left the yard without a deal being completed, then it would have been my fault, and I felt conscious of that.

Not long after this, the buying of bricks was arranged: deliveries would come by boat up the Wainway, once a week over three weeks. The heavy horses and wagons which came from Canterbury with the men would be taken to the creek. From there the bricks would travel to Midley by wagon.

We almost flew back to the Wainway, with both the tide and the wind in our favour. Once in the creek,

the boat pressed against the tide, but the wind still filled the sail, and we moved on at a good pace. The mood amongst us from Midley was mixed. We carried with us a sense of satisfaction that the church building could now progress, albeit with bricks alongside the cut stone and rubble. But my foolish adventuring up the stairs to the town could have caused more trouble than a bruised shoulder.

"They're like foreigners to us," Joe Rother said, "those men of Rye and Winchelsea. We can go there to trade, but there's no reason... none at all to go into the town. A dangerous place it is."

While feeling embarrassed that he had heard tales of me being caught up with the chase for Jem, I couldn't help but agree with his words.

# Edwin

My daughter is a woman now. I've known it for some time, but the arrival of these Canterbury men has made it clearer. I assumed she would settle for one of the sons from a local farm. Agney, Wheelsgate and Scotney have all produced men who know the Marsh and can provide for her.  But yesterday I saw how protective Diggory acted towards Gisella, and I cannot think of anyone I like better. In him I see a skilled man who is not afraid to take charge and lead men; a man who is fair and a man who is kindly.

Juliana has pointed out Diggory's thick golden hair. "It is wasted on a man!" she says with a smile. She has noticed that his skin is clear and his teeth strong. "I hear that his parents are still in good health."

My wife wants to learn about these men who are living in our barn loft, and it is no surprise that she has asked about their families. However, it is only now, after our trip to Rye, that I understand her meaning about his parents. Juliana knows that our daughter may leave Midley and travel further than Lydd or Romney. If she does, then Juliana wants to

know that Gisella is with a man who is not just kindly and hard-working, but who comes from healthy stock.

The plagues are no distant memory, passed down in stories through the generations. The black death swept through Romney Marsh when I was a boy of about Eliot's age. It took my grandparents and my sister in its wake, so when I think of Gisella marrying, it is no foolish thing to consider her future husband's health and of his parents.

Marrying! Here I am gossiping like an old woman. He went to her aid when the foolish girl ventured up those steps, and now I imagine her bags packed and her off to Canterbury. There is barley to harvest. I'll leave Juliana to these thoughts of our daughter's future.

# Diggory

My first thoughts of the day were about the drama on that cliffside staircase. *How is Gisella? Is the bruising worse?* My second were: *I wonder if they will return from the hills with the stone and wood today, or will it be tomorrow?* The delivery of the bricks is to be delayed so we can be sure of having our wagons back here.

As I left the loft for the site of our new church, I did not spot Gisella, nor any of her family. Part of me wanted to knock at the open door of their home and ask after her. I faltered, hanging back while the others walked ahead. *Stop it Diggory. You'll see her soon enough.*

Our days fall into a pattern where we work on the church for that short time after dawn when the dew still soaks the grass and leaves, and the air is fresh. Sometimes a low mist hangs over Romney Marsh. Then the sounds of the day are muted, and we are cocooned in our small world with its wooden church and the walls of the stone church rising.

When the sun has fully risen and the sky a clear blue, as it has been most of these summer days, we break our fast. This is a sociable occasion when we join the lay monks around the fire. We eat porridge with fruit and nuts gathered from the hedgerows. It is a time for us to discuss our plans for the new church. Everyone's opinion is valued here. A labourer may not have my skills, but they are learning about this land and this church, so their thoughts are listened to.

All the labourers have gone to Aldington and Bilsington, with two masons and a carpenter. We have been lucky with the carpenters – for now our need is men to dig foundations and lay stone, and these skilled woodmen have not objected to helping where they are needed.

"We can get on with building a church now," I reported as our depleted group met by the new foundation trench for the tower. "There's been too much uncertainty, with us not knowing what those back in Canterbury would want us to do. Now we know and will make the best of it. That wasn't fair, you having to re-work the tower trenches and chip all the mortar off the stone, but it's done now, and the new foundations can be laid."

"It will be a different place within a week," one of the carpenters replied. "Now we are done with the plan to have aisles, we can start on the nave walls."

"Then it will look like there's some proper building work going on," another answered, his voice full of approval.

"You know how to mix the mortar," I said to a labourer. "And you," I nodded to a carpenter. "Let's make a start on these foundations before we eat."

We set our own rules here at Midley. While the days are long and the sun beats down upon us, we rest after our midday meal. I prefer to separate myself from the other men and find a shady spot to linger for a while. It's a time when I become lost in my thoughts and often find myself dozing. Today I wandered along the rise in the land, where Middle Isle had once met the tidal waters of the Rother, and settled in the shadows of some gnarled thorn trees. From here I kept a look-out for Gisella and was rewarded when she appeared from the direction of Longhouse Farm with a basket in her arms. I stood and walked towards her.

"I've been worried about you," I said as we met on the open pasture. "How's your shoulder... your arm?"

"Bruised," she replied with a smile. "Mother wants to thank you."

"Thank me?"

"You saw off that... that man." Her expression sobered and she looked down at the empty basket. "I'm sorry. I'm sorry I wandered off. I thought..." But Gisella didn't say what she thought.

"Have you used a poultice?" I thought of my mother and her shelf of remedies in clay pots.

"Aye. The bruise is all black and purple but will soon heal."

I had an odd desire to lift her curtain of nut-brown hair, push aside her light tunic and see the curve of her shoulder... to kiss the bruise. Gently.

"No need to thank me," I said, recalling her earlier words and hoping she hadn't noticed me blush. "I just happened to see you were in trouble."

"Mother says you are to come to supper this evening – if you'd like to."

"I'd like to."

"We are always interested to hear more about Canterbury. The people who live there... the people who travel there. I know you have told us, but there is always more to learn."

"It's all so different," I began. How could I explain it to these people who knew so little about life beyond Romney Marsh? Only her brother, Bernard, had been to the city. "But I'll try."

She stood there before me, her expression curious, and I wondered if this young woman with her ready smile and her interest in my life... I wondered if she might, one day, come to Canterbury.

I ate well at Longhouse this evening. Fried fish with green beans and fresh peas made a welcome change from the inevitable broth served by the lay monks.

Afterwards, Juliana served cooked apples and blackberries with thick cream.

We did speak about Canterbury: the pilgrims trailing through West Gate, the death of Archbishop Sudbury which led us to wonder if more pilgrims would pour into the city and what, if any, miracles would be attributed to him. Juliana asked about my parents, my sister, and my brother Mark who was so against me leaving Canterbury. Sitting in their home, with the last of the sun's rays beaming through the window and doorway to the west, I reflected on my brother's strong opinions.

*You were wrong, Mark. It's not been easy, but the people here have welcomed us.*

I glanced at Gisella and saw she was looking at me, then I found myself turning to Juliana and said, "I've been telling you about Canterbury, but I've seen so little of Romney Marsh. I can see the old port of Romney across the fields. Perhaps on Sunday... perhaps Gisella can walk there with me?" I dared to look back at Gisella and saw her smiling her agreement.

# Gisella

These last few days have been busy for Diggory and everyone who is a part of building the church. First, the men returned from the hillside villages with fresh supplies of stone and wood. Then a boatload of bricks arrived, and every mason, carpenter and labourer went to unload it and stack the bricks on the wagons.

"It seems as if one thing after another has prevented us from building this church," I heard Diggory say to my father one evening. "But, at last, we have both men and materials here."

"Nothing will stop you now," Father replied.

"Nothing will stop us," Diggory agreed.

When we wander from the farm past the site of the stone church, we can see progress. The nave walls are now rising as a mixture of brick, rubble and flint. I have noticed that the bricks are both yellow and red in colour.

"They come from different places," Paul told me. "Before Rye, different places before Rye... "

I have noticed that the bricks, ragstone and flint are placed in the ever-growing walls in no order.

"It makes no sense to have one area of brick, one flint and one ragstone," Diggory explained. "If it fits then we place it there."

"Do you do this in Canterbury?" I asked.

"Canterbury has all the stone we need for each project," Paul told me. "It's different here. We've had to make our own rules."

Now they seem to work with an urgency that I've not seen before. In the first weeks, there was a sense of uncertainty... of delay, as plans were made and altered. Now they have the materials and a clear plan for our church – albeit a reduced church – and they work with a fervour.

"It's because they'll have to leave soon," Mother said to me.

"Leave?"

"Summer is over and the autumn equinox just days away. In another cycle of the moon, they'll be thinking about leaving."

"But so little has been done!"

"Which is why they work so hard now."

With these words on my mind, I met Diggory by the church and we set off along the track to the old port of Romney. A brisk breeze pressed on our backs, ruffling our hair and cloaks. It carried with it a nasty nip, reminding me that the long summer days were truly over. When we passed a lone beech tree, its leaves danced crisp and golden.

"Mother says you're making plans to leave."

"There's a lot of work to do before then." Diggory ran a hand through his golden curls. "Your father says that after harvest there will be men looking for work and we can pick up more labourers."

"You'll want to get home before winter sets in."

"We have to," he stated. "Will you miss us?"

"Of course. You can't imagine how quiet Midley is without you here – all of you from Canterbury. Weeks pass with no one new coming to the parish."

"How strange. All day long people pour into Canterbury."

"I'd love to see it."

"Would you?"

I fell silent, unsure of how to answer. Following the bank of an ancient creek, the track wound its way towards the old part of Romney, often called the old port. I began to worry what Diggory would think of the humble church, plain and irregular.

"We should have gone to the new port. It's further but the church is impressive... even you would think it was... at least I think..." I paused, uncertain of what he would think.

"I can see a magnificent cathedral or church every day once I am home. But look at this..." he waved in the direction of St Clement. "This is truly unique."

Then I remembered that he would have passed by on the way to Midley.

"We didn't stop." Diggory said as if reading my thoughts. "We were determined to reach Midley. Look at this tower – it's not at the west end as ours will be, but to the side. And the buttresses – I've never seen them so solid, so thick."

We picked up speed as we spoke of Romney – the old and the new – and tried to imagine the time when merchant ships sailed upriver from abroad with wine, materials and exotic foods, or down from the Weald with iron and timber.

"The Vikings came here," I told him with a sweep of my hand from the coast towards Appledore. "They say a Viking ship is buried under the church."

"Why? Why would they do that?"

"Perhaps it just happened to be there, abandoned, and they didn't move it. See how the land has been raised here? It's from when the ditches were cleared."

"And perhaps silting from the river."

"Maybe."

"So perhaps they put the spoils over the Viking ship? Just because it was there."

We crossed the Rhee by the bridge, pausing for a moment to watch its sluggish waters heading for the coast. Then Diggory and I were passing cottages and stopping to speak to the curious villagers.

"Gisella! Come to see your uncle?" someone called.

"After we've been to the church. If you see him, let him know."

"And who's this fellow with you?" another asked.

"Diggory Western, come from Canterbury."

"He'll be one of them working on yours then." The villager gave a knowing smirk.

"That's right."

Reluctant to linger, we were soon on the path leading to the church, then entering the shelter of the porch and lifting the latch on the old door. Silence wrapped itself around us as we stepped inside. The only movement came from the flickering flame in the sanctuary lamp. I stood for a moment, reflecting on the people who had worshipped in this ancient building over the years, and breathed deeply, absorbing the scent of old wood and stone.

I led Diggory to a chapel, and we stood by the tomb slab of an unknown crusader. "You've travelled from Canterbury to Midley," I began.

"And not even left the Kingdom of Kent, other than the time in Rye where I saved you from who-knows-what..." he continued, seeming to understand my thoughts. "How do they do it, these crusaders? How do they know where to go?"

"And what makes them so determined to spread Christianity that they'll leave their homes and families to go to lands where people have their own gods and their own ways?"

"We'll never know."

We left the slab, topped with a carved cross, passed through the nave and into another chapel. Here two faces were carved from stone either side of a window. Their sculpted hair fell straight and sleek, with immaculate curls resting against their necks. The pair had a sense of serenity about them, lacking etched creases and lines which would have given them a personality.

"Are these like... Do you have these in Canterbury?" I asked.

"Hundreds of them!" Diggory grinned. "This pair must be people from this place. They are beautiful."

"I believe they are Bertha Beaumont her husband, Clement, who put money towards this church."

"They probably paid for this chapel," he said. "I expect they lived nearby."

"Probably. Have you ever carved a face?"

"No." Now his voice was almost a whisper. "But I will one day. If... if I can work as a master mason on the cathedral."

"I wish I could see it," I replied, my voice also hushed.

"I hope you will."

With that, Diggory turned away from the stone faces, led the way through the nave to the porch and back outside. We circled the church, pausing to examine the window mouldings... the stout buttresses... the view across the fields to Hope. But

although the autumn sun shone upon us, the light began to change and we spotted grey clouds thickening to the west. "They'll be heading this way," I said. "They usually do."

"I know!" Diggory responded. "I'm getting used to the Marsh and the direction the weather comes from. But I must meet your uncle before we leave."

Reaching out, he offered his hand, encircling my fingers in his which were so much larger and rougher. Hand in hand, we left the churchyard and followed the track taking us to the road.

I steered us up the Ivychurch road before allowing my hand to drop away from his. "Just a quick greeting. He's along here." I spotted the old man shifting wood at his log pile. "Uncle! Do you need some help?"

"Nay, girl, I'm done here. I'll be heading back in." He turned and gave a toothless smile. "Who's this young man?"

"It's Diggory who is building our stone church."

"Oh aye, I've heard all about that. Greetings to you."

"And to you," Diggory replied. "I hear you're Juliana's uncle. She's makes us very welcome at Longhouse."

"Juliana's a lovely girl," my uncle said, his voice soft as if remembering the time when she lived nearby with her parents and sisters. "She came to see me just a few days ago. I live alone now."

"Eliot will be along tomorrow," I told him. "There's a fence that needs mending, so Father says. He'll bring a meal for you both."

"I'll be grateful for both the company and the food." Uncle glanced at the sky to the west. "I'd invite you in for a drop of ale, but there's rain due."

"I know. We need to get back."

We exchanged a few more words and then left. On reaching the bridge across the Rhee, Diggory took my hand once more. We spoke little on our return to Midley; it didn't seem necessary. My hand remained in his until we neared the parish boundary. The rain clouds had moved steadily across the sky, their pace faster than ours. By the time we walked up the rise in the land and were back in Midley, rain fell steadily, and we scurried along, hoods up and trying to avoid any puddles on the track.

Nothing could dampen my pleasure. Even now, when I lie on my bed and think of the day, I can feel the pressure of Diggory's hand wrapped around mine and the pressure of his thumb in my palm.

# Diggory

Three weeks have passed since Gisella and I walked to the old part of Romney. Today we set off to the new part. I have heard the church is magnificent, the designs influenced by our great cathedral, and I wanted to see it before leaving for Canterbury. The stone faces we saw in St Clement's were beautiful but crudely carved, and I was eager to see if the masons at St Nicholas showed greater skills.

But first let me tell you about the church here at Midley. As Edwin said, there is less work on the land now. Men have emerged from the farthest reaches of the parish to labour with us. Although not skilled in the laying of bricks and stones, they can lift, carry, and mix mortar, so we six masons can work without stopping to do the rough work. The labourers who came from Canterbury have been learning from us these past months, and every one of them can cut a block from a piece of rough stone or lay a row of stone and brick. We masons cut and shape the corner stones, window ledges, mullions and lintels, as well as building walls. I feel confident that the walls will

151

be built to full height by the time we leave. Meanwhile the carpenters are shaping wood for the main beams and trusses, as well as ensuring that the scaffolds are safe. As the church rises, we need more of those scaffolds and the platforms are raised every few days. The walls now reach to nearly six feet and the sills for the nave windows are in place. These windows are no more than lancets placed up by the eaves, destined to be left unglazed. Harry speaks of making shutters for them, most likely on our return in the spring.

Today, Gisella and I left Midley before our midday meal and set off in the direction of St Clement's Church. This waterway, the Rhee, which flushes out the harbour, makes it impossible to take a direct path to the coastal area of Romney. It must be crossed by bridge at the old part of Romney. We walked at a fair speed, knowing it was some distance to the new part of the town. Passing St Clement, we took a track known locally as Wallingham.

"This takes us past where the lepers used to live," Gisella told me, her tone unsure.

I squeezed her hand. "People use this track every day. And they are gone now? It's in the past?"

"It is."

"Shall we sit here and eat?" I asked, pointing out a fallen trunk. "What's that over there?"

"It's called Hope – a small place." Gisella eyed the potential seat. "It's damp."

"Your mother gave me a cloth to sit on!" I grinned, while reaching into my bag to extract bread and cheese. We settled on the trunk, our backs to Midley and facing Hope – an odd name for a place. The rough brown of my tunic settled against the green of her woollen dress, and I pressed my thigh against hers. It felt good to be close to Gisella.

We didn't stop for long before continuing along the Wallingham trackway. Once on the outskirts of Romney, Gisella suggested that we follow the old riverbank. "It will take us to the coast and from there the track leads straight to the church."

The church had been teasing me for some time and, as we neared it, the details of its stocky tower became clearer. We reached the coast, and my attention turned to it. A deep beach of sand and shingle stretched out to a distant sea. "Low tide," I said, unnecessarily, mesmerised by the movement of the distant water.

"You saw the estuary at Rye – you sailed on it," Gisella pointed out. "But this is different, isn't it?"

"I'd have liked to see it at high tide," I replied.

"Another time?" she suggested.

"I'd like that."

Hand in hand, we walked along the beachfront track. The land swept out to our right, encompassing the Norman church, and the coastline continued out

of sight. To our left, I spotted cottages and shacks, sheds and taverns. On the beach, capstans and ropes awaited the fishing boats. I took little notice of all these things; St Nicholas church dominated the view and my attention.

"Is it what you expected?" Gisella asked.

"I didn't know what to expect," I admitted. We stopped and I drank in the details, from the Norman doorway with its chevron carvings, to the round-topped windows, all rich with early 12th century detailing. "See how it changes here? The fashions have altered while this tower was built..." I pointed to the third, fourth and fifth layers, where the windows now boasted gothic points. Beyond that, four pinnacles completed each corner, and a stone spire rose between them.

"Why are they different?" Gisella pointed upwards.

"The pinnacles? Perhaps they reflected the tastes of different masons, or the person who paid for them." I placed my hand on her shoulder. "Look at all the faces, way up there. All those characters looking out over the town, along the coastline or out to sea."

"Will they be local people?" She nestled closer to me.

"Probably, but others too – the King and Queen from the time and other important people."

"The Archbishop of Canterbury?"

"Maybe."

Our attention turned back to the doorway and the land around it. "You know why it's higher here?" Gisella referred to the swathes of shingle which had been swept back to allow access to the church entrance.

"The storm? The great storm we learnt about." It wasn't just part of the story of Romney, but Midley too. We men from Canterbury had been told about how it affected the isle on that first evening when we sat around the fire outside Longhouse Farm.

"They say the tide flowed twice." She waved towards the beachfront track. "It came up here, destroyed all the homes and boats and flooded the town. Hard to imagine now, isn't it?"

We stood contemplating the force of the sea and the destruction. On this dull day, with the tide far down the beach and the breeze unusually light, it was easy to forget how wild the sea could be.

"Shall we walk around the outside?" I asked, pulling on her hand a little.

At the churchyard wall, we stood with our backs to St Nicholas and gazed across to where the shallow waters in the haven mingled with the deeper sea. The horizon blurred – grey sea against grey sky. I would have expected nothing else on this cloudy day. Turning, I found myself admiring the magnificence of the church and saying to Gisella, "It's wonderful. Thank you. Thank you for coming here with me today."

"I'm glad we did," she said, her response simple. Gisella led me towards the east end where she pointed out a tiny window. "It's for an anchoress," she explained. "There was one here once, before my time. But they still speak of her, and her likeness has been carved inside."

"Who did she pray for?" My gaze roamed around the churchyard.

"Someone who died that night of the great storm."

We pondered on this for a moment. I could see the eastern wall had been repaired and Gisella confirmed that it was damaged during the storm. More carved faces looked along the coast towards the boat repair yards and the track to the next settlement.

Entering the church through a doorway in the tower, I felt an inevitable sense of awe. In the nave I immediately spotted Canterbury's influence in the form of alternating octagonal and rounded columns. My gaze moved upwards to Norman arches, their decorative details cut into Caen stone.

"Is this what you want to do?" Gisella whispered. "Carve like this?"

"It's what I yearn to do." She stood so close to me that her shoulder touched my upper arm. Our fingers linked, and I could smell the lavender on her skin. It was time. Turning to face her, I took both her hands

in mine. "Gisella, my joy... marry me and come to Canterbury."

"Canterbury?" she echoed.

"I can't leave without you..." I faltered. "I love you with all my heart."

"I'll marry you." Her response was brief, but, like her, perfect.

# Edwin

Midley is subdued. The days are noticeably shorter, and we have suffered from a week of relentless downpours. The men from Canterbury think of the tracks across the hills to their home, knowing that, with every day that passes, their journey home becomes more treacherous.

Only my daughter, Gisella, glows. She is to marry Diggory. Although I know so little about Canterbury, I do know Diggory and give them my blessing. Juliana and I have asked just one thing from them – that they marry in Canterbury. We want our daughter to see the city before they commit to setting up home there.

"She can stay with my aunt," Diggory told us, "while I find us a home. She'll be amongst my family and friends."

It is all agreed. When the men return to Canterbury, Gisella, Bernard and Frank will go with them. Bernard and Frank will stay to see Gisella and Diggory married and settled in a cottage, or at least plans in place for their own home. This way, Juliana and I will be certain that our daughter is happy while we wait for the long winter to pass. In the spring,

they will return to us and work on our stone church will resume.

"If Gisella is unhappy, then we can stay on Romney Marsh," Diggory insists. His love for her makes anything possible. "There will always be work for a mason. I would walk to Ivychurch and work on their great barn of a church if it pleases her."

# *Diggory*

We are to leave our church within a week. Winter is nipping at our heels, and Canterbury beckons. Although I wish we could stay until the work is completed, mortar will not set as the temperature drops, our working days are becoming shorter, and the men are restless. Midley does not offer the entertainments they are used to. Besides, it was always understood that we would return to the city for the winter.

Although I speak of wanting to stay, I have good reason to long for the return to Canterbury. Once Gisella has seen the place, we will marry. There will be no delay! As I work, I picture us walking through the city gate, hand in hand, our hearts brimming with love and hope for the future.

None of the church is roofed, the windows are unglazed, and the interior is bare. The tower is not yet built, but the walls of the chancel and nave rise to a height of twelve feet. Tie beams, strong and straight, span the width of the church, but the carved king posts and trusses are not yet in place. Instead,

they rest against our walls of stone, brick and flint. Stone blocks are in piles and will remain untouched until our return when their sides will be straightened and corners sharpened, before becoming all-important buttresses.

We masons feel a pride in our chancel window with its three slender openings and the gentle curves as the mullions rise to a point. The other windows are no more than a row of squat lancets, three on each side, positioned at head height. They are placed to allow light into the church and may never be glazed. Sometimes we wonder what Archbishop Sudbury would think of our humble efforts, but what can we do when no guidance comes from Canterbury?

Overall, we are satisfied. In the height of summer, we left Canterbury with thirty nobles, twelve were lost, and the steward disappeared with two more. Despite these setbacks, we are building a church!

This morning, as I rummaged amongst the ragstone, I came across a great prize. "What's that?" Paul asked.

"Caen stone," I murmured, running my fingers over the gritty surface. "Caen!"

"How can we have missed it?"

"I have no idea." My fingers tingled and my heart glowed. An idea began to form.

"Can't do much with one piece," Paul commented.

"I can! I can carve a face and put him or her up there, so he or she looks down on the people of Midley after we have gone. We gazed up to the incomplete west wall, due to be finished within the next day or so.

"Who will you carve?" Paul asked.

"It should be Archbishop Sudbury," I replied without hesitation. "But I'll call a meeting after supper. This is not my choice to make. Edwin and Father David must come as it will be their church after we have left."

With our bellies full, we lingered before the fire this evening in the company of the priest and Edwin. Other names were suggested, and we pondered over Brother Fabian, the lost steward, or Prior John from Canterbury. Should it be someone from Midley, we wondered – Edwin, the reeve, or some character from the history of the parish? But, mostly, we returned to Archbishop Sudbury who had come to Midley and planned a stone church. We discussed his features, recalling him as a thickset man with bushy eyebrows and a wide nose. Although we mulled over other options, the decision to have the image of our murdered archbishop carved in this superior block of stone was agreed.

All day I have been drawn back to that piece of stone. I run my fingers over it and picture the archbishop's

features forming under the blade of my chisel. Tomorrow I will begin, and I am determined that, before we leave for Canterbury, the likeness of Simon Sudbury will gaze from the west wall and along the nave to the chancel window.

# Gisella

I wanted to marry before we left Midley. To walk to Canterbury as man and wife and to share a bed wherever we stopped on the way. Our church may be humble, but I could picture our union being blessed by Father David in the porch and the whole community celebrating with us. Now I cannot imagine what it will be like… where we will marry… the faces that will be looking on.

I'll know soon enough. We are to leave for Canterbury at daybreak. For now, I lie awake in my bed, listening to my mother's gentle snore and my father's snuffles. My space within my curtained area is pitch black, but dawn will come, as it always does.

# Gisella

## Canterbury

It took four days to walk to Canterbury. We made quite a procession – the lay monks, the masons, carpenters and labourers, Frank, Bernard and me. At times, the roads were slippery and hillside tracks treacherous, but the men felt pleased to be returning to their homes. They sang as they strolled along and pointed out familiar landmarks. Tales and memories were exchanged, and much laughter shared. Even Bernard recognised some of the places along the way, being no stranger to the route. I remained full of eagerness to see Canterbury and felt joy in the knowledge that Diggory and I would marry within days.

So firm was my belief in Diggory and our perfect union, that I had allowed our passion for each other to overcome me before we had left the Marsh. "We are to marry anyway," we told each other. "There is no harm in pledging our love." He gave me a simple band of woven grass, and we became man and wife

under the shade of a willow tree at the bottom of the hill which leads to Bilsington.

How wrong I was! How wrong we were! Now I am in Canterbury everything has changed.

We arrived late yesterday afternoon. My first glimpse of the city came from a hilltop after a steady upward trudge along the old Roman road. The sun shone weakly in a near cloudless sky, and I almost gasped to see the warm yellow of the cathedral towers... the nave... the chapels... Even from a distance, its splendour silenced me. The cathedral stood alone in its glory, yet not alone. Beyond its boundaries, buildings crowded against each other and a forbidding city wall encircled them all. Beyond these walls and gatehouses, roads trailed outwards, with cottages in clusters, churches and barns.

The very sight of the city invigorated us all, and we beat a steady pace to Worth Gate. Three of our men peeled away, taking the horses and wagons to local farms. The rest continued until the immense city wall towered above us, grey and – dare, I say it? – threatening. Not only was it high, but thick enough to resist an enemy assault, and wide enough for men to walk along its top.

"Did you build any of this? Can I see your gate?" I asked Diggory.

"Nay. My part is over there." He gestured to the west.

We entered through the city gateway and immediately I felt as if all that was fresh and pure in my life had been sucked out of me. The foul odours, the filth, houses jostling for space overpowered me. Shrinking away from it, I turned to my brother. "You didn't say it was like this."

"I did," Bernard retorted. "Perhaps you didn't listen."

A wave of nausea passed through me, and I felt as if I had shrunk into a paler, weaker version of myself. A group of women brushed past. I pressed my sack of precious belongings closer to me.

"You'll get used to it." Frank had moved so he walked beside me, a barrier between Bernard and me and the city people.

"It scares me," I whispered, immediately feeling disloyal to Diggory who was so eager to show me his home.

"Diggory will look after you. He has skills and will earn good money. He needs a little time but will provide you with a good cottage."

"I know." *But can he give me clean air and pure water? It feels as if the plague is brushing against me.*

"You know why Bernard and I came with you?"

"If I change my mind..." I began.

"You don't have to stay."

*But I do,* I silently screamed. *I have pledged my love. We are husband and wife now.* The band of woven grass pressed against my finger. I didn't reply

to Frank because, if I had, then I would have asked him to turn about immediately and take me back to Worth Gate.

Several of the men left us, striding into side streets amidst declarations that we would all meet again soon. The road turned a little, and I could see glimpses of the cathedral. It pulled me onwards, compelling me to stand before its glory. My spirits lifted.

"This way…" Diggory placed a hand on the small of my back and guided me into a narrow street. The cathedral was lost.

Then it began, a dizzying journey from street to alleyway, from patches of open ground where chickens pecked and dogs roamed, to priory walls, churches and chapels. Narrow bridges crossed a slow-flowing brown sludge of a river where the hardiest of hovering insects buzzed in the last rays of the day's sunshine. Our group dwindled until it was only me, Diggory, Paul, Frank and Bernard.

I saw a substantial church, not pale yellow like the cathedral but grey, with parts encased in scaffold towers. Then, beyond it, I could see snatches of city walls and a huge gateway.

"West Gate!" Diggory exclaimed.

"Your gate." Here it was – one of the places that I had been so eager to see. I felt nothing, none of the awe I had expected. My anticipation had been replaced with a sluggish feeling.

"You're tired," Frank told me.

I frowned, not knowing how he understood.

Then a new emotion came to me – shame. I didn't know where Frank planned to stay, but I did know that he had no family in the city. For four days we had journeyed together, and I thought only of myself. One moment he walked with us, the next he said, "Farewell. Keep safe until tomorrow." Then to me, his voice low, "Bernard and I will stay here for two days, perhaps three." Another of our group had gone.

We turned into a road with a tavern on the corner and three cottages, each separated by an alley.

"We're back!" Paul called.

As afternoon blended into evening, everything and everyone became muddled. The parents... another brother and sister with their children and spouses... an aunt who I was to stay with, and a neighbour who may or may not have been a relative. Questions... The sharing of local news... We ate with bowls on our laps, not all, but some of us. Stifled by the air, thick with woodsmoke and body odour, and the people whose voices vied with each other, I smiled and nodded but found myself increasingly lost.

"It's great, isn't it?" Diggory placed his arm around my shoulder. "I'm so glad you are here meeting everyone."

Everyone. Who were these people? Which one was his sister? Was that an uncle or someone who

happened to be passing by? Darkness wrapped itself around the cottage, but not the pure blackness I knew from the night sky above at Midley; this was a cloudy... a smoky... a dirty, stifling blackness.

"You'll be..." a woman spoke to me, but her accent sounded unfamiliar and at the same time I was jostled from behind.

"I'm sorry... I'll be?"

"Staying with me... along the road here."

She must be the aunt, I realised. "Aye." I gave a weak smile. "It's kind of you."

Not long after that, we left – me, Diggory and the woman... the aunt. We passed the tavern and turned into a wider road. None of it was familiar to me, especially in the darkness.

"Here we are." The aunt pushed on the door of a low cottage and stepped inside. I faltered, knowing I should follow but unable to see any more than the outline of her body. "That's better." Diggory's aunt returned with a lamp, and we stood at the doorway, the three of us, with our faces illuminated by the weak light. "You'll be wanting to stay?" she stated, looking at Diggory. "To lie with her."

He frowned and his eyes flicked towards me. "Nay, we'll marry within the week and then... then we'll set up home somewhere."

"But you've already pledged your love," the aunt insisted. "She wears a band. It's only grass, but a band nonetheless."

I looked down, wanting to avoid her scrutiny.

"We'll be together soon enough," Diggory answered. "My parents are expecting me."

With this he left. I was shown a pallet on the floor and the bucket in a rough shelter just a few steps from the back door. I would have loved to slosh cool water over my face, to plunge my arms into a basin of warm water scented with lavender or rose, but this was not offered. I merely thanked the aunt for her hospitality, removed my shoes and outer layers of clothing, and unrolled my blanket.

Now I lie on the thin mattress, the slats of the pallet digging into my shoulder and hips, my blanket wrapped tight around me. I can hear the scurrying feet of a mouse and people talking as they walk along the street.

My thoughts wander, as they tend to, while I drift off to sleep. The part-built church at Midley... the bustling city streets here in Canterbury... the lost monk... my family... our journey across the Marsh... They merge and mix until none of it makes sense.

# Gisella

I woke at dawn, my head aching and mouth dry. Footsteps could be heard on the street and the rumble of a cart. Slight vibrations passed along the earth floor and through the pallet to my aching bones. The aunt snored. I hadn't thought to ask if there was an uncle, or any other person living there. Easing myself up, I sat on the edge of my bed and looked around the space, but the light was still too dim. I lay back and fell into a deep sleep.

The next time I woke, the aunt was awake and shuffling about by the fire. "It's been a while since I had company," she said. "I didn't like to disturb you, but I've got work to do." She nodded towards a loom and a couple of large wicker baskets which I hadn't noticed the evening before or when I had woken at dawn.

"I wouldn't want to delay you," I said. "I'm grateful for a bed. Perhaps I can help? Later..."

"Perhaps you can, but you'll be wanting to see the city first and meet the priest."

"The priest?"

"You're getting married, aren't you? Properly this time."

My head still ached, and I longed to rinse my mouth with some freshly drawn water from a well. A memory of last night's brief conversation came to me – this woman knew that Diggory and I had already pledged our commitment to each other.

"Aye… we are." I stood with my blanket around my shoulders, then swiftly changed it for my dress. "I'll go out to the… the bucket. Could I have some warm water? We were four long days walking here and I long to wash away the dust from the roads. I have some scent to add to it."

"I'm putting some on to warm," she replied, while placing a small iron pot over the smouldering fire. "I thought you'd ask. There's a bowl over there… behind the screen. It will be ready when you're back."

Rubbing my forehead, I thanked her, thinking that everything would seem better when my skin and teeth felt cleaner. The headache would ease, and no doubt Diggory's aunt would offer me something to eat. Then he would arrive and show me the city. I reached for my bag and withdrew a smaller package containing my linen rag and pot of ground sage with salt for cleaning my teeth, and some oil with lavender to add to the water for washing. But first the outside bucket…

While I sat on a stool eating porridge, Bernard arrived. "Diggory told me how to find you," he said.

"Is that where you're staying?" I asked, my head still muzzy.

"Nay, I'm with Mark, like before. What's wrong with you, Gisella?"

Had I felt better, I would have laughed to hear his frustration. But my spirits lifted to see my brother. From the moment we stepped through the gate and into the city, I felt that I had no friend here. But, for now, I had Bernard.

"It's all so different, and my head aches."

"Come with me," Bernard replied. "I'll show you the West Gate that you've heard so much about and then the cathedral. The fresh air will do you good. After that Diggory will be ready. We'll meet him at the cathedral."

I picked up my cloak and tied my purse to my belt, then thanked Diggory's aunt for her hospitality. With my heart feeling lighter, I stepped out into the street.

*Fresh air! Can't he smell the rotting waste that lines these streets?* I pulled my cloak over my nose and mouth while stepping around the ale slops outside the tavern. *Only a downpour could give me some respite.* We walked along the centre of the street, the gutters being filled with things that I didn't like to examine closely. But when a cart laden with wood passed by, we were forced to step to the side. Now I had to try my best to avoid food waste, faeces and pools of urine.

"Doesn't a cart come to collect this waste?" I asked Bernard, his days here with Frank making him wiser than me.

"Sometimes they don't come soon enough. Depends on the size of the families."

We approached a pile of something tasty enough to attract a couple of dogs who snapped at each other while gobbling the feast. I looked up to see a sign telling me this was a butcher's shop. Vomit rose in my throat, and I quickened my pace, back towards the middle of the street.

"Move out of the way!" Someone bellowed. We stepped into a side street as two men marched along carrying a bier with a covered body on it.

"Come on," Bernard said. "Just along here and we'll be on the main street that goes from east to west."

The road became wider, although still crowded, and relief flooded through me. I let the cloak fall back into place. We passed a hospital – a kind of hostel where pilgrims are welcomed and able to rest, Bernard told me. Then I glimpsed the river, spanned by a wide bridge that formed part of the main street. Curious, I looked down, then grimaced. They say our many ditches on Romney Marsh are stagnant and unhealthy, but this shallow river moved along sluggishly, thick with waste. No wonder when the gutters in the streets all led to it – at least that is what I believed.

"Do you think Frank is staying there?" I asked Bernard, and we glanced back to the hospital.

"I'm not sure. He's not a pilgrim. He had some place to go though." Bernard pointed forward. "Now, look at this, Gisella. You'll be cheered by West Gate – I know you will!"

My brother was right. To see this gateway that the Westerns had worked on for so long that they took their name from it... To think that my Diggory... my husband had learnt his trade while placing stone upon stone. We had passed through Worth Gate yesterday afternoon, but this was far sturdier, taller and altogether more impressive. As we neared it, I paused and stood, taking in the details – Gothic pointed arches, a castellated top, sturdy buttresses and curved mullions.

"Let's walk through." I smiled at Bernard, encouraging him.

We stepped into the shadowed interior and across the drawbridge.

"Another river!" I commented.

"The same one," Bernard told me. "It splits and joins again." What a lot my brother discovered on his previous time here!

Once more I paused and gazed at West Gate, in awe of the immense turrets rising from the ground to the battlements.

"We need to go to the cathedral," Bernard reminded me. "Diggory will be waiting."

Retracing our steps along the main street, we could see to our left the cathedral towers and rooftops rising above the homes, taverns and shops. My headache forgotten, I felt eager to view this holy edifice – the grandest building I could aspire to see in my lifetime. We passed the hospital and reached the road where Diggory's aunt lived, but now turned to face the cathedral. Once more it became obscured by the buildings crowding a narrow lane and, once more, I pulled my cloak to cover my nose, as the stench was unbearable.

The lane was, thankfully, short, but the memories of it stayed with me. We entered a small market area, barely paused, and strode through the entrance to the cathedral grounds. Now I saw it in all its glory – the cathedral that had captured Diggory's heart.

"It's too much," I whispered. "How am I meant to know where to look?"

At that moment Diggory came bounding across the green. Sweeping me into his arms, he swung me around in a circle. "Gisella, my love, I have been offered a job!"

"Here? On the cathedral?" I asked. "It's what you've always wanted."

"I've hoped for it for years."

"Where will you work? Which part?"

"Here! Here on the nave." Diggory gave a sweep of his arm from left to right. "I'll do whatever they want of me."

"And they'll wait... wait until you've finished our church at Midley?" I paused, noticing the glee leave his face. "Or... or let you go back for the summer?"

"Nay, the stonework is mostly complete at Midley. There's no need for six masons next summer; it's carpenters they need next and experienced tilers."

*He's not going back to Midley. We are not going back to Midley.*

I glanced at Bernard whose stricken face showed that I had not misunderstood. I could not expect my brother to fight my battles. "Bernard, do you mind if Diggory shows me his city... his home. I'd like to see the places which are special to him. I'll see you later."

"Aye, we are to eat with my parents at noon," Diggory added. "Do you know your way there?"

"I know it," Bernard replied. "I'll see you later."

"Let me show you our cathedral." Diggory took my arm and led me towards the western end with the double towers. I cannot call it the tower end because there is another in the centre. Three towers!

I craned my neck, looking up and up: niches with lifelike statues, canopies of stone carved to look like fringes of material, a window both tall and wide with mullion after mullion soaring upwards to a gothic point. Buttresses. Pinnacles. Decorative details with no other purpose than to scream: *Look at me! I am the greatest cathedral in this land!* I felt both awestruck and repelled, for this is the place which

meant Diggory would never truly be mine. It is his first love and his greatest love. I said nothing. Words could not express my confusion.

Taking my hand, he led me inside. We paused once more. My gaze followed the pillars up and up to the vaulted ceiling – vaulted with stone, not wood. *How can this be possible?* To each side of me, aisles stretched the length of the nave and windows gleamed, ablaze with colour. The painted stonework depicted both ordered patterns with vines and flowers, and scenes with characters. All freshly painted within the last few years, by order of Archbishop Sudbury. This was his vision, along with our humble church.

The archbishop's reconstructed nave was not yet complete. In its lofty heights, artists painted and masons chipped away, while glaziers fitted delicate glass.

"Isn't it magnificent?" he murmured.

I was about to reply when I noticed them... the pilgrims. They had been there all the time, but my attention had been on the lofty extravagance.

"Where are they going?"

"Down to the crypt where Thomas Beckett was murdered," Diggory told me. "We are used to them here... I'm used to seeing them trail through West Gate and along the main street. When I'm here, I'll get used to them being about the place."

"Where will they go afterwards?"

"They follow each other to the new chapel behind the high altar. I'll show you, but not now. There's plenty of time."

"What's in the chapel? His tomb?"

"A casket of gold, set with jewels. The visitors will lodge in Canterbury for several days. They'll buy badges, and ampullae filled with holy water. Pennies, grouts, and quarter nobles – that's how the money comes to Canterbury."

I tried to imagine it but floundered. How could I when my experience of the world is so limited. For a moment, my mind became filled with the wonder of both the cathedral and those people who made the pilgrimage here. Then it came flooding back to me – Diggory had no intention of returning to Midley. Our plans had been changed in an instant with no thought to my home or family.

Suddenly I felt stifled by it all. "Can we go outside?"

"Of course." He looked at me, confusion on his face. "Don't you like it?"

I turned towards the doorway. "I love it, but I thought you wanted to complete our church at Midley. We are returning there next spring. My parents are expecting us."

We stepped out to the cathedral grounds, moving away from the flow of pilgrims.

"We'll send a message with Bernard. No one would expect us to return now I have this chance to

be a master mason on one of the greatest buildings in England."

"My parents expected it, and so did I."

"Come on, Gisella. Come and see my city."

He squeezed my hand, smiled, and I saw my Diggory. I recalled his words: *'If Gisella is unhappy, then we can stay on Romney Marsh'*. He had been overcome by the thought of working with Caen stone and making his mark on the cathedral, but later he would remember that his love for me was greater, and one more summer in Midley could do no harm.

Hand in hand, we followed the lanes towards North Gate. They were no cleaner than those I had walked earlier, but I felt more protected with Diggory beside me. He stood between me and the carts that passed by, and his instincts told him to be wary of an open doorway through which a bucket of waste could be thrown. The cry 'mind the water' often came too late! From the gate, we followed the city wall through orchards, herb gardens and small vegetable plots, and it would have been pleasant had the river flowed pure and clear. *What stench will erupt from the Stour when the summer sun beats down upon it?*

Cottages, workshops and the inevitable taverns sprung up once more as we neared West Gate. Pausing often, Diggory pointed out the parts of the gate and city wall he had worked on. Our route took us past Holy Cross church where we saw his brother, Mark, at work.

"Where will we live?" I asked. "When we marry?"

"With my parents, now my sister has her own place. But not for long, I have saved every penny and grout I earned, and we'll have our own cottage."

"In these streets, near your family?"

"We all live here in this quarter... all of us. It's our place." Diggory paused, then continued, "Perhaps you'd prefer somewhere different, but I think your parents would like to know my family are close by."

*I don't know if I can bear it here. Will I find that in a week... a month... the dirt, the stench, no longer bothers me? That I can learn to accept it?*

"Can we live outside the city walls?" I asked.

"We can. But it's not where the Westerns live." He frowned, unable to picture a life beyond the walls.

"And where will we marry – here at this church?" I looked towards Holy Cross.

"We go to St Mildred's. I'll take you to meet the priest tomorrow afternoon. My mother has arranged it."

I pondered on whether I had seen St Mildreds. Most likely I had. The priories and churches melded, one after the other, in this city.

We reached the short lane of three cottages, but rather than go to the front door, Diggory led me down the alley. "Come and lie with me, Gisella. In the storehouse."

"Your parents..."

"We are all but married by a priest. You wear my band."

I looked down at the ring of grass around my finger. "Not now, Diggory."

I have found my way back to West Gate, walked through it and across the Stour. The road led me to a church named St Dunstans and a place where the air is purer. Canterbury attracts and repulses me. The cathedral, the city walls, the gate houses don't fail to fill me with wonder. But the stench, the filth, houses jostling for space, make me long for Romney Marsh. I must turn about now. The thought of entering the city makes my body heavy, and I am certain that I will never love it as Diggory does.

# Gisella

"What do you think of Canterbury?" Diggory asked as we walked through Newingate and past St Augustine's priory. We were heading for the Saxon church, St Martin. "This place is rich with tales from the past, isn't it?"

"What do I think?" I had spent my second night on a pallet on his aunt's floor. It was comfortable enough, and I woke feeling much better. Today we would speak to the priest, and I was determined to see the best in Canterbury. "What do I think? There's so much of it... so much more than I could have imagined."

"I understand, but it will be quieter over the winter when the pilgrims stop coming. Even now there are fewer than in the springtime."

"You need them to bring money?"

"We do. How else could we pay for all these repairs on the cathedral?"

We had walked up a rise and Diggory pulled on my arm; we turned and gazed back at the cathedral. Clouds shrouded the sun and the buttery yellow of

the Caen stone was dulled, but as we stood, a shaft of light burst through, lighting the east end.

"It has the power to pull people to it," I told Diggory. "Within its precincts, more people live and work than in the whole of our parish at Midley. It is a city within a city."

"It pulls me to it," he agreed. "And now... at last... I can work on it, learning new skills and leaving my mark for the centuries to come."

We continued walking, reaching St Martin, a small plain church. I knew I must talk to him about Midley and our plans to return there. All this talk of the city and the cathedral brought us no closer to speaking of the important things.

"Did you tell them... the cathedral masons... about your plans to return to Romney Marsh in the spring? That you planned to see the church finished?" I asked.

"Why would I when I had this offer?"

"Because that was what you had planned."

Diggory grinned and turned to place both hands on my waist. He planted a kiss on my lips. "Let's not harp on about that, Gisella. Not now you have seen my city."

"But if Midley is not good enough... not grand enough, then what about St George at Ivychurch or St Nicholas at Romney?" I stayed in his grasp and gazed up into his clear blue eyes, no longer liking what I saw. "You said to my father that you'd

willingly work on either of those churches, and I'm sure they would be glad to have you."

He kissed me again. "But it's not the same, is it? You can see that now."

"I can see it," I agreed. "The sun is high; we must return as your mother is expecting us."

We spoke little on the way back. For me, there was nothing more to learn about Canterbury or Diggory. As we approached Newingate, I found the courage to voice my thoughts: "Diggory, you promised me that we would return to Midley, but now you say we are to remain in Canterbury. You must stay, but I must return home. Today."

"Oh, come on, Gisella. You will become used to the place and perhaps we'll have our own house built of stone. Anything is possible now."

"You can do all those things, but not with me. I need to find Bernard... or Frank."

He pulled me into the shadows of the city wall. "You made a promise. You pledged your love. We are as good as married. We'll marry within days, and you can choose where you want to live. Outside the city walls if it pleases you. Dunstans... that's the place where Harry is and it's not too far from the cathedral."

A home outside the city walls would have suited me well. But something had shifted between me and Diggory. The cathedral was his greatest love, and I hadn't known it before.

"You changed our plans. If God is disappointed with me, I will face His judgement when I pass from this life." I broke free from his clasp and pulled the ragged grass ring from my finger. The strands fell apart. "I am going to see your mother, to thank her for welcoming me."

"There's no need. We can think of a way... A visit. We can visit Midley."

"People like us do not go about the land visiting. There will be work to be done on the cathedral and a home to care for." I took a few steps, and he followed. "I'll go alone."

"You don't know your way."

"I'll find it."

Tears began to form, and I turned away. *How can my feelings be so changed within days?* I felt sick. *Just walk, Gisella. Walk towards West Gate, then down the lanes.*

Luck was with me as I recalled that Frank had a day's work in the orchard between the West and North Gates, so rather than go straight to Diggory's mother, I sought him out. Our conversation was brief. "I'm leaving with you and Bernard. But can it be today? I know you have planned for tomorrow or the next."

Frank showed no surprise. "It can be at four when my work here is done. I've left nothing in my lodgings and can meet you at Postern Gate." He

glanced at his canvas bag slumped on the ground by an apple tree.

"Thank you." I tried to push aside my concern about what little distance we could cover by leaving so late in the day. "Do you know where Bernard is?"

"Aye, he's with Mark at Holy Cross."

"I'll find him, and we'll meet you at Postern. I mustn't stop you from working." I paused, unable to imagine how the three of us would fend for ourselves that evening. "I'll buy some food. Frank, I'm grateful for this. For you coming to Canterbury with me and not asking questions when you're told I must leave. Thank you."

Tears welled and, before he had a chance to reply, I had fled.


Bernard showed none of Frank's foresight and was surprised when I told him our plans had changed, but he agreed to meet me on the main street, near the pilgrims' hospital. "I have to see his mother and aunt, then I'll be there," I said.

"We were to eat with them," Bernard pointed out.

"Not now. We'll manage on our own. There are plenty of stalls selling food."

With my heart in my mouth, I dashed to the Western family home, and then to the aunt's cottage. My apologies and excuses were brief. When I left with my blanket roll in my arms and a canvas bag

over my shoulder, my body felt lighter than it had since entering the city gate only two days ago.

I didn't see Diggory again.

Frank looks after us well. As I reflect on the day, we three are bedded down in a stable loft with a simple meal of bread and cheese inside us. This farm lies just beyond the city, and they took us in without too many questions. Tomorrow we will continue walking as far as we can, finding food and shelter along the way. I can hear my brother snoring, but I think, like me, Frank is still awake. No doubt he feels the responsibility for both me and Bernard. I wonder what he thinks about as he drifts off to sleep. I wonder how far we will walk tomorrow. I wonder what Diggory is doing and thinking… My body feels heavy. I will sleep soon.

# *Juliana*

## Midley

My daughter has been home from Canterbury for these past three weeks. Although Edwin and I had worried about Gisella living so far from home, we trusted Diggory to care for her. But no sooner was he back in his city than he chose the cathedral over Gisella and our stone church. We did not expect that of him. For days it was all we spoke of, but time passes, and we find we are accepting that they will not marry. In the spring, Diggory will not return to complete the stonework.

As we enter the shortest days of the year, I have a new worry. Gisella has not suffered her monthly bleed and these last two mornings she has been nauseous. She picks at her food and her skin is pale.

I have not spoken to Edwin about my fears but I have a plan.

"Frank, can I walk with you? I'd like to visit my uncle." I fell in step beside Frank as he left Midley for

the old part of Romney. Recently, I had arranged that he would go to my uncle's smallholding most days to help where he could. Uncle becomes frailer by the week and although a woman cooks for him, tends to the washing and mending of his clothes, and keeps the hearth swept, a man is needed to care for the land.

"Of course. I'd be glad of the company," Frank responded.

"Are you comfortable in our loft?" I asked. Since the other men left, we had invited Frank to stay with us.

"I am. It's strange though, isn't it? Just me."

"We'll get used to it. All we think of now is keeping warm and fed over the winter. It's a lonely time. I hope you don't regret staying here."

"I won't. It's good of you to offer me this work."

We walked on in silence for a few minutes, my head spinning as I tried to find the right words. In the end I just blurted them out: "Frank, you like Gisella, don't you? Would you marry her?"

"Like Gisella? If she wanted to marry me then I'd be the luckiest man hereabouts, but she didn't choose me, did she? What's this about?"

His reply was blunt, and I couldn't blame him. "She *needs* to marry."

We walked the length of a field before Frank spoke again. "She wouldn't want to return to Canterbury? To Diggory?"

"Even now, Gisella will not marry unless she loves and is truly loved in return."

We walked on and had almost reached the bridge over the Rhee when he spoke again. "We walked together for four days, from Canterbury to Midley, and in that time she put all feelings for him aside. She did not say it, but it is what I believe."

"Bernard thinks a lot of you."

"He is the young brother I never had!" Frank grinned. "But we are speaking about your daughter – is this her idea? For me to raise another man's child?"

"It is my idea. We have not spoken about it... marriage or the infant."

We crossed the bridge and once more silence fell between us. Frank ran his hand through his hair and turned to face me. "Juliana, you cannot expect me to answer now. Let me think about this – and it is not just about having a wife and child. How am I to care for them?"

"Here! Here in Romney," I told him. I had planned it all. "My uncle has no children and he adores Gisella. He is an old man who would welcome you both. No one will know about Diggory. No one will know."

"I'll tell you something, and I don't need to think about it," Frank answered. "A home and a job are something I pray for, but not forsaking Gisella's

happiness. If I agree, and she agrees, it will be because it is right for both of us."

"I know that, Frank. That is the reason I choose you to marry her."

I spent a while with my uncle speaking about the years gone by, then drifting towards the present. "Thank you for sending Frank to me," he said, as he does every time now. "If my sons had lived, then I would have been glad if they had been as cheerful and willing to work at any task." Uncle has reached a great age and has been on his own for a long time now.

"He is glad of the work," I reminded him, "and likes it very much here."

I didn't see Frank again before I left but know he will ponder on my unexpected offer, and I trust him to make the right choice, even if it is not the choice I asked for.

Once I am back home, I will not say anything to Gisella about the baby or my thoughts about her marrying. If I wait, then I am certain that gradually everything will come right for my family.

# Gisella

I am to marry Frank! It surprises me still, but it is all agreed!

A week ago, he found me standing alone on the 'nose' of Midley, my back to the stone church. "Gisella," he said, after apologising for startling me. "You and I have become good friends."

"You are the best of friends," I said. But despite these joyful words, my voice sounded dull and my spirits were low. Nausea had become my constant companion and, with it, a weariness like none I had known before.

"Can you tell me what's wrong?"

"I can't tell you."

"Then how can I help?"

I frowned, because I believed no one could help. I said nothing and expected him to go away, but he didn't. Even when it began to rain, he didn't leave but led me to the shelter of the wooden church. He knew me too well to take me to the stone one. And then, even when the rain didn't ease and dusk hung over

Midley, he stayed at my side despite my giving him no encouragement.

"I am with child," I blurted out. *Now he will leave me in peace.*

"Then I can help," he responded without hesitation. "We can marry."

"But it is not your child!"

Then I laughed for the first time in weeks. I laughed and laughed until I coughed and was forced to run from the church to vomit on the grass outside. We walked to the well by Longhouse and he produced a bucket of cold water for me to dunk my cupped hands and drink from them.

"Thank you. I feel better now."

"I meant it, Gisella. Marry me and no one will know whose child it is. Marry me and I'll look after you. I have work with your uncle, and we can make our home in the old part of Romney. It's just over there, across the fields. Near enough to your family, but far enough from..."

"From him... from the memories," I added.

"We'll make new memories."

"Everything has been so awful," I told him. "Let me think about it. A day. Perhaps two?"

I said nothing about this to my family but thought about it all night and through the next morning. In the afternoon I set off towards Romney, where Frank

had gone to work, and met him midway between there and Midley as he returned before dusk.

"You have an answer for me?" he asked.

"Are you still offering to marry me?"

"I am."

"Then I'll accept with gratitude."

An awkward silence followed. He reached for my hand. "Gisella, you must know... I need you to know that I have admired you all the time I have known you. I thought Diggory was the best man for you. But I was wrong."

"We were both wrong," I gazed into his pale blue eyes. "It will take time for us to get used to each other, but I think... nay, I am certain you are the better man."

He grinned, and I liked the way his freckled nose creased. "Do we seal this with a kiss?" Before I could reply, he brushed his lips lightly on mine.

We walked back to Midley, not full of plans for the future but in near silence. I think we were both wondering what would happen next. Our words came in short bursts.

"It will have to be soon," he said.

"I know. People will gossip."

"They always gossip!"

Then a while later, I asked, "We need to speak to my parents. I haven't told them about the... the baby. There is no need now."

"Perhaps you'll find that your mother already knows?"

And when I found myself wondering where we would live and how he could provide for us, he reminded me, "Your uncle needs to have someone with him. The house needs repairs, and he is lonely. I think we can make our home with him, if that suits you?"

"It would suit me very well."

As we approached Longhouse Farm, I wondered, "Will you mind that the child is not yours? Will you be able to love it?"

"It will be your child, so I will love it," came his immediate reply.

It seems as if a month, not a week, has passed since those awkward talks with Frank. Mother has been to-ing and fro-ing a lot, making sure the cottage at Romney is thoroughly clean and supervising the building of the bed, including the hanging of curtains to keep the warmth in over the coldest months. Pots and pans have been sent to the smithy for repairs and the thatcher has been hired to patch the roof. We are days away from Christmas and a brisk wind has whipped across the Marsh for this past week, yet everyone works to make a home for Frank and myself.

Mother says nothing when I am sick in the morning, but she offers me rosemary tea and is

frugal with the spices in our food. I am certain she knows I am with child and that Frank has saved me from a life of shame. Yesterday, he moved from our barn loft to my uncle's home, so I may not see him again before the wedding.

As for the wedding – it is to be held at St Clements. Frank suggested, and I agreed, that we would like to marry where we will live. What we didn't say is that at St Clements we will not be in the shadows of Diggory's church. It marks a new start for us both. I hope for this dreadful wind to stop gusting across the Marsh. When frosts come and the ground freezes, it will be both prettier and easier to travel from Midley to Romney. I pray for my sickness to ease, and for Frank to see me glowing from the walk to church, not pale with shadows under my eyes.

I will love Frank and be a good wife to him, because I know that he will stay true to me and the child.

# *Diggory*

## Canterbury
## 14th June 1382

The city of Canterbury is my place. My home. When I dust myself down at the end of the day, I feel proud to be a part of its story. Where I once worked in Kentish Ragstone, I now chip and carve in soft Caen. My master says I have a rare connection with the stone and has given me the most prized task – to carve a likeness of Archbishop Sudbury's face and a shield with an image of his hound. My fingers tingle at the thought of beginning this job, and I study the sketches daily.

Today we were ordered to place our tools at our feet and stand in silence, whether that be on a scaffold or the floor. I stood up high on a wooden platform by the north wall and watched as the mayor and important figures from the city joined Archbishop William Courtenay, Prior John and numerous priests and monks. Led by a priest holding a cross, they

proceeded to the tomb of Archbishop Sudbury, now topped with a brass and copper effigy, and an ornamental canopy. Once out of my sight, they began to pray for his soul, their voices rising and falling in harmony.

My thoughts wandered to that tiny settlement on Romney Marsh, the lost nobles and the stone church. I wondered how Harry Woodman was progressing with fitting the rafters and ridge beam and if Frank had remained in the area or returned there in the spring to meet the Canterbury men. Or had Frank, like me, chosen a different path? I remembered the one piece of Caen stone found amongst the grey ragstone and my first attempt at carving an image of the murdered archbishop.

Inevitably, Gisella came to mind – that wonderful woman, full of confidence and so interested in life beyond Midley. I let her down badly. I became a man possessed by my passion for this cathedral and could not tear myself away from it. *What is she doing now? Does she think of me?*

# Gisella

## Midley
## September 1382

Today I walked to Midley for the first time since my son was born a month ago. My husband, Frank, strolled beside me, Theo in his arms. He is the best of husbands and the most devoted father.

The men from Canterbury returned to Midley last spring, the old team – Diggory, Harry and Frank – much diminished. Only Harry was left to lead the men both living and working in Midley, while Frank walked there several times a week to help the lay monks with their duties. This new arrangement ran smoothly, with most of the stonework already complete and the carpentry taking priority. Over the spring and summer, the roof rose and wooden shingles were nailed in place, until inch-by-inch the chancel was covered and they began on the nave. Before this had been completed, and the buttresses built up to the eaves, my body became so heavy with

child that I decided to remain at home with my dear uncle.

The old part of Romney became my world. Before long, Theo was born and all my attention focussed on him. Suckling the infant and the constant changing of the swaddling cloths filled my days, alongside feeding my menfolk and keeping the fire smouldering.

I must return to today and that first visit after the birth. My emotions flitted from an eagerness to be home with my family to a sensation of unease at taking Theo to the place so closely linked with Diggory. Would the people of Midley recognise his features in the shape of his face or the blueness of his eyes. I mentioned none of my fears to Frank, but I think he sensed my unease.

The stone church has become a clear landmark when walking the track to Midley. Inevitably, as we strolled towards the village, my thoughts roamed to last summer and Brother Fabian who lost those precious nobles. No one ever heard of him again, and we never tired of wondering what had happened to him.

"Do you think they will send anyone to see the new church?" I asked. "Anyone important?"

Frank knew that I referred to Canterbury. "I think the first they will see of it will be when Archbishop Courtenay tours Romney Marsh."

"There will be no special visit?"

He shrugged. "Who knows what them in Canterbury have planned. They share none of it with Harry or your priest... or anyone here."

"It's too far away," I mused. "Perhaps the farthest parish from Canterbury."

The prior seems to have lost all interest in our stone church and Archbishop Sudbury's plans for it. Not that we truly know what he thinks. All we know is that no more nobles have been offered and, as long as the church is built, it seems that Prior John and Archbishop Courtenay will be satisfied.

The coloured glass in the chancel window, the shape of the tower, the simple patterns painted on the plastered walls... they can all be chosen by the people of Midley, with Father David making the final choice.

Frank and I walked mostly in silence, comfortable in each other's company and pleased to see Theo settled in his arms. We paused once to change the swaddling cloth and for the infant to suckle, and soon after met with my mother who had come to join us. Before long, the track sloped upwards and we stepped onto the sandy 'nose' of Midley and headed towards the wooden church where the rest of my family, villagers and church builders gathered for mass.

Falling into the familiar routines, a feeling of peace settled on me while listening to the readings

and prayers. I breathed deeply, taking in the scents of incense and ancient timbers.

"Come to the stone church with me," Mother said afterwards. "Come and see the changes."

I trailed after her, thinking that I would prefer to go to Longhouse and sit for a while. "Just a quick look," I replied. "Theo will need to suckle again…"

Inside everything seemed fresh, new and unfinished. The shell of the building was complete, but the embellishments had barely started. "They are looking for old glass to make up this window," Mother nodded towards the chancel window, the only one to have any grandeur in its design. "The others will be shuttered only."

"That's how it has to be."

"They won't plaster until the spring," she told me. "And then, when it is fully dry, we can all take our part in decorating the walls of the nave. Father David will no doubt find someone to paint the chancel."

"Will they come from Canterbury to plaster?" I adjusted the sleeping infant, moving the weight from one arm to the other, but that felt awkward so I asked, "Can you hold him for a moment?"

Mother took Theo and answered while rocking him gently, "Nay, I think local men will plaster the church. When the Canterbury men leave the church will be blessed and we can use it. As for its being consecrated… we will have to wait for word from Archbishop Courtenay"

"And a bell?"

"There is no money left for a bell, but if Canterbury can provide one, then the structure is in place to hold it."

We wandered to the far end.

"Harry and the others have done a fine job." I ran my fingertip over a carved feature on the pulpit.

Theo snuffled and I turned back to my mother who was standing in the shaft of light beaming through the unglazed chancel window.

"He has Frank's hair," Mother murmured, running a fingertip through the fine hair on the infant's head. "Your father's mother and brother were redheads too, thankfully. But no one will think of that when they see the resemblance with Frank."

Our precious infant has surprised us – his fine hair has an obvious tinge of auburn when it catches the light. "I'm glad of that," I responded, weary from the walk to Midley, "Glad for Frank."

"It's transformed," Mother said in an apparent change of subject. "The screen... the roof..." She waved her hand in the direction of the decorative rood screen separating the chancel from the nave, then towards the rafters now fully covered in wooden shingles. "It is all about the carpentry now, Gisella. It is almost as if..." She glanced towards the lone stone face, gazing over our heads towards the chancel. "... as if *he* was never here."

*You are wrong. Diggory's mark will always be here in this stone church. But when I return to Romney, then it is just Frank with me and Theo.* "Let's go back to Longhouse." I walked through the doorway to the slim tower and out into the autumn sunshine.

# *Joan and Phil*

## Somewhere on Romney Marsh
## October 2018

"You'll never believe what I've just found!"

"What's that?" I, Phil, straightened my back, removed my headphones and walked towards Joan.

"Fragments of a medieval coin. Two bits. Just a spade deep." She gave them a gentle rub with her fingers and the sandy soil fell away. "It's fake. See how the gilding has worn. Twenty-five years looking for a hammered gold coin and I've found a fake!" Joan laughed. "I'm going to see if I can find any more."

"I'll come over and help you look." We had been detecting in different areas but now I joined Joan.

We replaced our headphones, adjusted the detectors and returned to the same hole. Joan's detector immediately gave a signal, and two smaller fragments of a gilded coin were revealed.

Another beep. "I'll dig for this one," Joan said, reaching for the shovel. "Here it is."

"A gold coin this time?" I grinned.

"Not likely! I think it's a..." Joan brushed earth and grass roots from a decorative metal bar. "A cross – a cross Pattée. Looks like it was part of something else. It's broken."

I took the find and raised it, so the sun caught its ancient curves. "It's old," I murmured. "A fourteenth... fifteenth century purse bar?" I passed it back to Joan. "Interesting."

We resumed our positions on the field. Headphones on. Detectors poised.

Within a couple of steps, I was alerted to something else below the surface. Gingerly, I removed the top layer of the soil, then a little more.

Something glinted. It shone as only gold can shine when lifted from the earth after more than six centuries. "This isn't a fake. It's real!"

# Emma

## October 2018

Today I popped round to see Joan and Phil. "We found something yesterday," Phil said, producing a plastic pot. I have several the same in my plastics drawer in the kitchen. His had little packages of folded tissue inside.

"Joan found this." He unwrapped the first tissue. "It's a fake gold coin. You can tell it's a fake because of the tarnish. Pure gold comes out of the ground as bright as bright can be."

*That's interesting.*

"Then I found this," Joan added, unwrapping the next find. "It's a broken purse clasp." We looked at the clasp, examining the break and the ancient metalwork.

"Then this." Phil revealed a gleaming gold coin and placed it in my hand. Lightweight and thin, about the size of a two pence piece, the craftsmanship was incredible. Before me there stood a King aboard a ship, a sword in his hand and a shield protecting his

body. I could see his hair, his crown, the detailing on his armour and on the ship. Encircling the image were words in a language unrecognisable to me.

"It's beautiful," I said, my words inadequate.

But Phil was busy unwrapping the next folded tissue, and the next...

"We've been detecting for twenty-five years," Joan told me. "This is what every detectorist dreams of."

"Five gold coins," Phil announced as the final coin was placed on the coffee table before me. "Five gold coins, the fake and the broken purse clasp."

"That's amazing." Again, my words seemed inadequate.

"And you're the third person to touch these in over 600 years," Phil said.

That was the moment when as I realised how significant this find was. I felt a shiver run through me.

# *The end*

# *Thanks*

Thank you to everyone who supports my writing through buying my novels and attending workshops, and to the local stockists.

I am so grateful to those who spend hours helping me with the editing and proof reading. Every error you spot helps me to improve the final draft.

Many thanks to my friends and family who are so understanding about the huge amount of time I need to spend creating novels, workshops and talks.

# *Midley*

Midley – The Settlers
Lydd & Midley 11th century
(2024)

Midley – Five Gold Coins
Canterbury & Midley 14th century
(2024)

# *Coming up...*

Midley - Abandoned (working title)
Brookland, Midley, Old Romney 16th century
(estimated publication summer 2025)

Midley – At War (working title)
Lydd & Midley 1940s
(estimated publication autumn 2025)